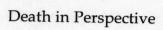

Death in Perspective

Death in
Perspective

Joan Lock

To Audrey
With all the Best.
Love.
Joan Lock

November 2001.

ROBERT HALE · LONDON

© Joan Lock 2001
First published in Great Britain 2001

ISBN 0 7090 6818 2

Robert Hale Limited
Clerkenwell House
Clerkenwell Green
London EC1R 0HT

The right of Joan Lock to be identified as
author of this work has been asserted by her
in accordance with the Copyright, Designs and
Patents Act 1988.

2 4 6 8 10 9 7 5 3 1

Typeset by
Derek Doyle & Associates, Liverpool.
Printed in Great Britain by
St Edmundsbury Press, Bury St Edmunds, Suffolk.
Bound by Woolnough Bookbinding Limited.

1

The silence was the thing which struck Jenny the most and which she liked the least. It blanketed the house, filling every nook and cranny with an almost pulsating tension. She knew she was being ridiculous; that she probably felt like this only because it was so isolated, so hidden away. Why would anyone want to live in such a vulnerable house – so far from fellow human beings and help? But that, madam, she told herself firmly, is something to which you are just going to have to become accustomed.

'Forget the past! Forget the past!' she lectured herself out loud. 'Things are going to get better from now on!'

No question, the view through the kitchen window was sublime, she thought, dragging herself away from dark memories. The endless lawn was dotted with circular beds of cheerful and delicate early spring flowers. Not solid blocks of the crude, cadmium yellow, giant *King Alfred* daffodils but a glorious mix ranging from the all white, *Snowball*, to the soft *Golden Ducat*, punctuated with spears of the crisper, snootier narcissi in all its forms. Behind the thatched garden shed to the right she could just glimpse the tops of apple and pear trees in the orchard beyond. Attractive as it all was, she decided, the view would need some rearranging for her purposes. Instead of marching stiffly across the centre of the lawns the path would be made to slant, meander even, towards the garden shed which, in turn, would be moved even further to the right. She could see it now.

But, before all that, she could put it off no longer, it was house-inspection time.

The pale-green hall was dominated by two large portraits. The one to Jenny's left was of a languid young lady, in a long and clinging lime-green dress, lying back nonchalantly across a rose-patterned chintz sofa. Probably 1930s, judging by the bias cut of the dress and the way her black hair clung to her head in deep Marcelle waves. The other portrait was more formal. A man of about thirty, in army officer's uniform, standing upright beside a leather Queen Anne armchair. His right hand, which he held stiffly across his body, clutched a swagger stick. More difficult to date this one. No fashion give-aways apart from slicked-down hair and pencil moustache, but there was a ready-for-action look about him so, Jenny decided, he would probably soon be off to fight in the Second World War.

'Did you ever come back?' she wondered. 'And if you did, were you all in one piece?'

Of the two rooms flanking the hall the larger one proved the more cosy. It was lined with books and furnished with well-used armchairs facing the discreetly cupboarded television. The smaller room was more formal. Roses again on the chintzy sofa and armchairs but these blooms were full blown; alongside, dainty, spindly-legged tables scattered with small, choice objects and curios. This would be the reception room. Everything seemed in order in both.

Despite her nervousness, Jenny was beginning to relax, but when she placed her foot on the first stair a sharp crack rang out making her jump with fright. 'It's only old-house noises,' she told herself sharply when she had stopped shaking and was breathing normally again. That's what Robin would say. 'Creaking floorboards and shifting foundations, they all have them. It's quite normal, bumpkins.' And he was right. But what if some nutter had seen her coming down the lane on her own? It could happen! She was a sitting duck! It was all very well for men to be so sanguine! Don't be ridiculous, she told herself, get a grip. You'll frighten yourself to death ten times before you actually die if you carry on like this.

She had calmed down considerably by the time she had checked that all was well in the green and gold master bedroom; a frothy pink and white, single bedroom and two more masculine, sporty lairs. Indeed, she was quite enjoying herself as she always did in this initial poke around. Only one more room to go.

She reached out and grasped the worn and dented brass door-knob, turned and pushed. Nothing happened. Stiff, obviously. Grasping harder she turned more firmly. Still no joy. The knob turned all right but the door refused to open. One of those handles which needed jiggling. She jiggled and pushed. No response. She pulled the door towards her and turned, pushed it away from her and turned. It made no difference. The door was well and truly locked. Now, why would that be? The answer was, it shouldn't. Odd. Very odd.

'But nothing to get in a state about,' she muttered grasping her hands together to stop them shaking so much. She had been doing too well. Why did he have to be away right now! But no, insisted the sensible voice-over she had been bringing in ever since the nightmare happened, this was *not* a bad omen. Nor was it a sign that something sinister lurked beyond. It was a locked door and there were any number of innocent reasons why it should be so, the main one being someone had merely forgotten to reopen it before leaving. No problem. No problem at all.

Detective Sergeant Bridgeman contemplated the sulky girl sitting opposite him. He was sick of sulky kids, particularly those like this one who seemed keen to give him a glimpse of their knickers. He concentrated on his notebook.

'So, you don't know why she told her mother she was staying at your place?'

The girl pushed back her hair, pouted and shrugged casually. Enjoying herself no end. 'Nah,' she said eventually.

'This *could* be serious.'

'Yeh,' she nodded. 'But she's gone before, hasn't she?'

He sighed. 'Yes, I know that, but we still have to make enquiries.' He wanted to say that he couldn't care less where the silly little cow had gone. He could have said, yes, she's gone before but not *quite* like this. 'So there was nothing odd – unusual – about her on Thursday evening?'

'Nah.' Mandy's pale blonde-streaked hair flopped over her eyes. She dipped her head forward then flung it back, patting and stroking the hair as it fell into place – for the moment. Why couldn't she pin it back or something! All this fiddling about drove him nuts!

'Had she any more money than usual?' he persisted. 'Was she wearing anything different? Did she seem nervous or excited?'

Mandy was becoming bored. 'Nah, nothing different.' Her glance drifted out of the window into the school playground where her mates stood gossiping in groups. She waved to one of them who giggled. The teacher who was sitting-in exclaimed, 'Mandy!' But she had to say it again before the girl turned back reluctantly to face Sergeant Bridgeman.

The missing girl, Linda Blackstone, had left home saying she was meeting her mate Mandy and would be staying the night at her place. The classic cover.

'Done that before, has she?'

'What?'

'Said she was staying with you, but wasn't?'

'How should I know?'

Bridgeman folded up his notebook. 'I think I'd better talk to your mum and dad.'

Ah, that had grabbed her interest.

'What for!'

It was the word dad that did it, he reckoned.

'To find out what more they can tell me about Linda and you.'

'Won't know anything I don't.' The tone was aggrieved but less belligerent and she had sat up and was looking straight at him, not out of the window or at her nails.

'Has Linda got a boyfriend?'

'No.'

That was a bit definite. He raised his eyebrows.

'Honest.' She hesitated, 'Well, no one in particular, far as I know.'

'Tell me what you talked about last time you saw her.'

'Oh, do me a favour,' she pleaded. ' 'Ow should I know? What did you say to your wife the day before yesterday?'

That was easy. Nothing. She'd walked out three months ago.

'Think!' he exclaimed, with a firmness that startled her and her chaperon. 'For goodness' sake girl, *just think.*'

She stared at him for a minute, unsure how to react, then began to talk. 'Oh, you know – about the fellas in form B1 – an' where we was going on Saturday night – an' she told me about her new dress.'

'She had a new dress? I did ask if there was anything different. . . .'

'She weren't wearing it, was she? She was *going to get it* – an' some shoes and a bag.' She paused. 'Well, what's weird about that? Got to get new stuff sometime, haven't you?'

Bridgeman knew that Linda's mother was a lone parent and that money was short. A new dress, shoes and bag all at once would do serious damage to a tight budget. But, he had to admit, Mandy had a point.

'Yes,' he sighed, 'you got to get new stuff sometime.'

Half closing her eyes to rid the scene of distracting detail, Jenny dipped her brush into a strong wash of burnt sienna, touched it here and there into the still-wet light underwash of raw sienna and brought the plant pots to glowing life. She loved doing that. It was like magic.

Reluctantly, she had shelved the task of mental path-slanting and shed-moving. The full garden view would have to wait. Instead, she was tackling what Robin had dubbed, 'one of your perfect potting-shed pics'. Perfect potting-shed pics might idealize the world of sometimes sordid soil-caked plant pots and dilapidated greenhouses, but they went down well with some of her customers. Particularly the upper middle class gardeners who adored all the business of selecting bulbs and seeds from colourful catalogues, transferring them to pots and trays, then nursing them along in cosy greenhouses, like the one she was sitting in now. The tougher, all-weather tasks they left to hired help. And why not? Doing what you wanted was what money was for. Her perfect potting-shed pics were reliable money spinners. 'Vital consideration, darling,' as even Robin admitted. 'Vital.' So, after she'd knocked off a couple of these, she'd treat herself to tackling the full garden view.

She poked in a little raw umber for the soil which could be glimpsed over the pot rims and was noting how the shadows fell beneath the smaller, primrose pots when the golden light abruptly deserted the scene. She glanced up accusingly, but the sun continued to shine down very brightly for the time of year. No clouds blocked its path.

She froze. Oh, God. Someone or something was just outside the greenhouse. Her gaze remained riveted on her painting and her hand refused to move. A gentle tap on the door forced her to look up. There stood a large, cheerful-looking young man with long, dark, curly hair. He wore navy-blue dungarees, an orange shirt and a beaming smile, gave a half wave and opened the door.

'Hi, I'm David, the gardener. Hope I didn't startle you.'

She struggled to keep the tremor out of her voice as she mumbled, 'Oh, no. Of course not.'

Gardener? Gardener? Her mind went blank. Was there a gardener? Yes, of course there must be a gardener in a place this size. Places as large as this usually had one. But surely he wouldn't come on a Saturday?

'Usually come on a Monday,' he admitted, opening the greenhouse door wider, 'but I've got something on then so I came today instead.'

He said it in an easy matter-of-fact way as though he was quite used to pleasing himself about these things. Reasonable.

It's *reasonable!*, her voice-over yelled. Does it matter which day you prune the roses for God's sake?

'Oh, fine, fine,' she said, as though she had been asked and thinking, I'm in a totally vulnerable position here. But she managed to keep her voice even as she murmured, 'I don't think Mr Furness left any particular instructions.'

'Oh, I know what needs doing. Bit of lopping, chopping and pruning today, I think.' He grinned at her. 'Technical terms, you understand.' Gazing around the garden he muttered, almost to himself, 'It's all looking a bit raggy around the edges.' He glanced over at her painting, 'Hey, that's not bad.'

'Thank you.'

'Looks almost professional.'

'I hope so.' Almost – what a cheek. She smiled. 'Just needs a few lost edges here, some colourful darks there and a general tweaking of tones. Technical terms, you understand.'

They both laughed.

The man was a charmer. No doubt about that. Eyes lit up reas-suringly when he smiled and all that stuff. All the more reason to doubt him, wasn't it? After nature-boy had wandered off in search of his technical aids she rose from her canvas chair ever so casually, picked up her water pot then sauntered easily back to the house. Once there, she thumbed feverishly through the pink notes. Yes, there it was. Just under 'ANIMALS: one six-year-old tabby cat, Hector. To be fed twice a day', she read, 'Expected callers to the premises: Gardener, David, Monday 10 a.m.–2 p.m. Will also change the duck's straw.' Well, that was something good, wasn't it? Save her a bit of a tedious and unpleasant task. She read on: 'Pops in for a cup of tea around 12.30 p.m.' Well, that was good too. If she could get him talking she might be able to satisfy some of her curiosity about Berry Hill House and its owners – while making it quite plain that Robin was due to arrive any minute.

Linda Blackstone's bedroom was immaculate. Some house-wifely tidying up had doubtless taken place before their arrival.

11

Bridgeman wished it hadn't. Clues and character hints may well have been swept away along with the dust. It was a typical young teenager's bedroom: posters of girl groups, super models and 'Boy of the Month' young soap stars. Piled up on a bedside table were *Missy* and *Mizz* magazines and over on the melamine dressing-table were tacky ornaments, half-used bottles of nail varnish, a giveaway teddy and a framed picture of Mandy and Linda messing about in a photo booth.

'There,' said Linda's mother. She held up a small, once pink, spotted stuffed dog. 'Linda would never have gone off without Raggy. She's had him since she was three.' Defeated would be the adjective Bridgeman would use to describe Mrs Blackstone. It was evident in the way she held herself, her lack of eye contact and her appearance. As though she'd tried very hard, then suddenly given up altogether. A thin, twitchy woman with densely black hair and red-rimmed eyes, she held her head down most of the time.

DC Carol Raycie glanced at Bridgeman before asking gently, 'Did she take Raggy last time she went?'

'I don't know.' The woman shook her head. 'I didn't check then, did I?' She twisted one of Raggy's back legs anxiously then seemed to rouse herself, lifting her head and making herself look them in the eye before saying challengingly, 'But it was different then, wasn't it? We *knew* she had gone on purpose. She left a note saying so.'

'Yes,' admitted Bridgeman, recalling that they'd never really got to the bottom of where Linda had been. She'd claimed she'd been to London and had been 'sleeping rough' but didn't have that typically seedy look which resulted from nights under the stars. Nor that sickly pungent smell of old sweat caused by lack of changes of clothing and bathing facilities. They hadn't pressed her. There seemed no point. She was back. She'd missed her mum and swore she'd never leave again.

'Is there anything else you think she wouldn't have left behind?' pressed DC Raycie. Obviously, Raggy alone did not make a convincing enough case for her, either, thought

Bridgeman. 'Make-up? Jewellery? Hair twisters?'

Mrs Blackstone gazed perplexedly at Linda's dressing-table and began picking up brushes and ornaments and putting them down again. 'You know what it's like. It changes all the time.' She hugged the scruffy toy to her and murmured tearfully, 'Only Raggy stays the same.'

In other words, like so many parents, particularly working single mums, she didn't really know what her daughter possessed or, come to that, what she got up to.

'Oh, don't I know,' said Carol, who had daughters of her own. 'Crazes follow crazes. Mine are currently into these new animal cracker ear-rings and bracelets. Can't live without them. At least I *think* that's what they're into now. Who knows, it might have changed by the time I get home tonight.' She paused. 'Tell you what,' she said, quietly continuing to search the dressing-table drawers as she spoke. 'Why don't we get Mandy around here to have a look? She might know.' She paused. 'You wouldn't mind, would you?'

'Oh no, anything. Anything to help get my little girl back!'

Carol nodded, 'She would know what the latest 'must have' was. What Linda and she couldn't live without.'

Mrs Blackstone held up her hand. 'Linda didn't have as much as the other kids,' she said apologetically. As she said it she caught sight of herself in the dressing-table mirror, was obviously appalled by what she saw and began patting pathetically at her hair.

'Of course not,' said Carol. 'We single mums can't keep up.' She paused. 'Mandy did tell us about Linda's new dress, though.'

Mrs Blackstone's hand stopped patting and her gaze transferred to Lindals reflection. 'New dress?' She was clearly perplexed. 'She didn't have no new dress.'

Bridgeman had reckoned on asking her about the new dress later. He had been holding it in reserve. But, what the hell. Now was as good a time as any. This was woman's stuff and Carol knew what she was doing. He gazed across at the other shabby council semis opposite. God, what a dismal place this was.

'She told Mandy she was going to get a new dress, shoes and a bag.'

Mrs Blackstone shook her head from side to side. 'No, no. She wasn't getting no new dress. She *wanted* one. She kept going on and on about this silver dress in Glad Rags' window. But I just couldn't afford it.' Tears were building up on her lower lids, 'I was even afraid she might steal it, she got so worked up about it!' The tears spilled over and ran heedlessly down her cheeks. She sat down on Linda's bed clutching the wretched Raggy to her and rocking back and forth looking to Bridgeman like a prime candidate for a nervous breakdown.

'Mrs Blackstone,' said Carol softly, 'I must ask you. In your description you said she was wearing a clip-on tooth brace.' She held the item aloft. 'Would she have left without it?'

The woman on the bed let out a moan, her hand went to her mouth as she gazed at the ugly, wired object. 'No!' she whispered. 'No! She hated the thing. But she wanted to be a model so she never left it off for more than an hour or two. She would *never* have left home without it!'

Close up, there was definitely something mesmerizing about David the gardener. Perhaps it was the rather odd combination of an athletic build, an open, almost childlike face with curiously wide-set dark eyes, and coal-black, tumbling, Pre-Raphaelite curls? Jenny was never quite sure about girlish curls on a man but they seemed to suit his nature-boy image. Dickon – that was it! He was like her picture of the primitive boy in *The Secret Garden*, only dark instead of rusty-haired and grown tall. Also, she had to admit, rather scrumptious.

'Do you mind?' he asked, as he made his way to the sink to wash his hands. Asking permission while actually doing something again, she noted. Admittedly, he was more of a fixture at Berry Hill than she but, after all, it was she who was in charge of the house.

'No, please go ahead,' she said a touch frostily. 'You'll find a towel over there.' She pointed to the Aga rail. He smiled slightly to himself making her blush crossly. So it was to be a struggle for superiority? Much as such tedious games irritated her, she was not about to concede easily. He was only a bloody, jobbing gardener after all.

'Coffee or tea?' He could hardly miss the icicles in her voice, now.

'Oh, coffee please. It smells delicious.' He'd got the message. 'Cut above what I'm usually offered, I'll tell you.' Don't overdo it, she thought. He dried his hands and very carefully rearranged the towel on the rail.

She passed him a steaming cup and indicated the chair opposite her across the kitchen table. He took an appreciative sip and exclaimed, 'Mmm. Beautiful. What is it?'

Jenny prided herself on her coffee. 'A Brazilian, dark roast.'

'Where from?'

'Waitrose.'

'Oh, I must get myself some of this.' He was trying hard. Well, at least that showed he had some sensitivity. Give the man a break. They're not all Aden Bullens.

She pushed some of her best oat biscuits towards him and, feeling slightly foolish, said, 'Been coming here long?'

'About a year.' Clearly anxious to get on a better footing, he went on to fill her in on his background, talking easily and, now and then, making her laugh out loud. She hadn't done much of that lately. It transpired that David ran his own gardening service as an offshoot to the small, organic market-garden business he was trying to get off the ground. A graduate of agricultural college, he had intended to go into farming, but didn't like the way things in that world were going these days and, at the moment, hadn't got the capital anyway. Organic gardening seemed to be a growth area, he murmured with an apologetic grin, but it was very hard work.

Not just a jobbing gardener, after all, Jenny chastised herself and anyway, what if he had been? She was no snob. No cause to be, goodness knows.

She had the urge to pump him further and perhaps bring up

15

the locked room, but sensed it was too early and besides she did not want to appear frightened or vulnerable. That deadly combination. So, beyond agreeing that Mr Furness was a nice bloke and David being grateful that the man 'left him to get on with it and just do what seemed to need doing' they left it at that. In any case, there was an etiquette to these things. Jenny had never forgotten the cleaner who had eulogized her employer to the skies on her first visit then, gradually, each successive time, dropped another little negative comment or casual acid aside about her until, eventually, the poor woman had become practically demonized. Of course, she shouldn't have listened. Particularly as, by then, Jenny had ceased to be curious anyway. The house had already become her own property again, as usually happened when she house-sat.

'So what d'you reckon?' Bridgeman asked Carol Raycie, as they fastened their seat belts and she gently let out the clutch. He felt comfortable with Carol. She was one of those plonks who, while not being exactly butch, was a little boyish with her crisp, short haircut; neat but very plain, plain clothes and straightforward manner. At the same time, she had a motherly air.

'I think she *could* have left her brace behind if she wanted to look good while she was with someone over a longer period and/or if . . .' – she paused as she stopped to make way for an elderly pedestrian – 'something better than the vague promise of modelling sometime in the future had turned up. Or again, she may have decided to leave on the spur of the moment – after some tiff with her mother.'

'Mrs Blackstone never mentioned any tiff.'

'Oh, believe me, they go on all the time. Who knows when real umbrage will be taken?'

'Hmm. Right.' He sighed. 'Girls.'

'They're such a pain, aren't they? In fact, there's only one thing worse.'

'Boys?'

'Right. Now *they* can be lethal.'

'What about the dress?'

Carol frowned, 'I'm not sure. Could have been romanticizing. Hoping to persuade her mum to buy her it for her if she wore her down enough. Or, as mum suggested, aiming to nick it. Or . . .' – she paused, before coming up with the real bad news scenario – 'someone *else* was going to buy it for her, for reasons best known to themselves.'

Just what he'd thought. The dreaded, mysterious someone else.

'What we need is more input from that bloody Mandy and her silly mates.'

'Yeh.'

'Good luck,' he grinned.

'Oh, ta.'

There was a short silence as Carol slowed right down before making the tight, left-hand manoeuvre into the station yard. Bridgeman broke it. 'You got a bad feeling about this one, too?'

Carol sighed and nodded. Every missing teenager could be her own Jackie or Bella and, who knows, it could be catching. 'After school that day she seems to have dropped off the face of the earth.'

'Better give that Mandy a good grilling.'

Carol smiled. 'I thought you'd done that?'

'No.' He sighed again. 'You know how secretive young girls can be.'

'Hmm?' Carol raised her eyebrows.

'Well, all right,' he admitted. 'I might not have handled her all that well.'

'Good grief! Can I have that signed in triplicate?'

'Nope. In fact repeat one word and I'll say you beat it out of me.'

'Tell you what, Detective Sergeant Bridgeman,' she said, patting his arm, 'you have gone up in my estimation no end.'

'Cheeky moo. Don't forget your upcoming review.' He got out of the car then bent over to speak to her again. 'I really do have a bad, bad feeling about this one.'

17

'Me too. Poor bloody Mrs Blackstone if we're right.'

'Well, you go and grill Mandy and put her on toast, and I'll spread the good news upstairs that my minor enquiry is showing distinct signs of turning into a major one. Then I'll follow up the one decent lead that silly cow Mandy did condescend to impart.'

2

Jenny was painting pots again. Big, fat, round ones this time.

Just as she was halfway through the tricky business of completing the background in one even wash, a technique which demanded carrying on to the end without stopping, she was disturbed again. Not by a shadow falling across the subject – this time it was the sound of heavy footsteps advancing up the path outside towards her which caused her to freeze mid-action.

'Don't be such a *wimp*,' she chastised herself. 'Look up. It's probably only the gardener again.'

A brisk, no-nonsense knock on the greenhouse door forced her eyes from her pots. Outside stood a tall, grey-suited man of about thirty-five. He knocked and pushed the door open.

'Hello. I couldn't get an answer at the house so guessed someone might be up here.' He reached into his inside pocket. 'You alone here?'

'No, of course not. My husband's just down there.' She flung out her hand to indicate the orchard, knocking over her water pot in the process.

'Oh, right.' The man brought out a small, folded card case. 'It's just that the house door is open. A bit dodgy that in such an isolated place, I thought.' He opened the case and held it towards her. 'Detective Sergeant Bridgeman, Birchfield CID.'

Jenny gazed at him, stunned. 'Oh God!' she exclaimed, when she found her voice. 'Robin!' She jumped up, knocking over her canvas stool. 'What's happened! What's happened!'

19

He held out his hand to steady her. 'Nothing! Honestly, nothing! This is just a routine enquiry.'

She stared at him for a minutes, then looked down. The water was spreading over the picture she had been working on all morning, tinting it a dirty brown with the scraps of soil from the bench. Then, she burst. 'Are you insane!' she eventually yelled at him. 'You stupid sod! You scared me out of my wits and now you've ruined my picture!' She righted the water pot and furiously banged it down on the bench.

For the first time he noticed the water dripping through the bench slats. 'Oh, sorry!' He fished out a large white hanky and made as if to dab the paper but she stayed his hand. 'No! Leave it!' Picking it up she held the paper at an angle until most of the water had dripped off one corner. She perched it, slanting, on a sill. 'What is it you want, for God's sake!' She was near to tears.

'I'm sorry, Mrs Furness, a girl has gone missing and—'

'I'm *not* Mrs Furness.'

'Oh,' he said, and glanced towards the orchard as if for help.

'And my husband is not down there, either.'

'Oh.'

'I made that up because I thought you were the mad Birchfield rapist!'

'Right. Sorry. I should have phoned, but I was just passing nearby and—'

'May I see your card again, please?' she snapped.

She held it in her shaking hand and read it slowly and thoroughly, but how was she to know whether it was a fake or not?

He handed her his mobile. 'Phone my office if you like. Ask them for a description.' She waved it away. She was being ridiculous. Hector suddenly appeared and began rubbing up against the sergeant's leg. He bent down to stroke the tabby and looked up at her confidingly. 'I've been having a bad day. Can I go out and come back in again?'

She began to smile despite her fury. She took in his square jaw, thinning fair hair and intense grey-blue eyes. Quite nice really.

He shook his head sadly. 'Not done a thing right, yet.'

She gave him a don't-give-me-that-sob-story look then turned her eyes to heaven for strength.

He contemplated the ruined painting guiltily then enquired, 'Isn't that what they call the wet-in-wet technique?'

The cheeky sod. She laughed out loud.

Had Bridgeman been present he would not have recognized the girl who sat opposite DC Carol Raycie. Mandy's hair had been tied back neatly as if to signal her new attitude which was alert, attentive and even marginally helpful. Carol might have wondered what Bridgeman had found so difficult about the girl had she not been aware of the mercurial quality of teenagers and how the attitudes of witnesses could change once the seriousness of the situation got through to them. Maybe a parent or teacher had rammed the message home. Instead of having to drag things out of Mandy, Carol had to stem the flow of information to keep it coherent and make sure she missed nothing out. Firstly, she needed to establish whether Mandy was, indeed, the fount of all knowledge concerning Linda, or whether there was someone else they should be onto straight away.

Slightly offended by the suggestion, the girl exclaimed, 'Nah, we was best mates!'

Past tense. Or just bad grammar?

'You did everything together?'

'Yeh, almost.' She hesitated. 'Well, pretty well everything. We didn't stick like glue or nothing. Couldn't really 'cos Linda often had to go off.'

'Go off?' asked Carol patiently, thinking, God, give me strength.

'Yeh, you know.' She had become monosyllabic again now that Carol was controlling the information flow.

'No, I don't.'

'Well, she had a couple of jobs, didn't she?'

'Right.' Carol waited. Mandy was a nice-looking girl when she stopped pouting. Lovely grey, catlike eyes, a slim and elegant face with a slightly large but very straight nose. Almost aristocratic until she opened her mouth. Then it was the ugly, harsh tone rather than the accent which jarred. Eventually, Carol's patience was rewarded.

'She baby-sat a lot 'cos they didn't have much money. Oh, an' she did a bit of cleaning.'

Past tense again. 'Where, exactly, did she do the cleaning?'

'Oh, like I told the geezer' – she caught Carol's look – 'the sergeant – out at that house behind Pennymead. Creepy place, she said it was.'

'Why creepy? In what way?'

'Down this lane, you know. Right out of the way. In the country. Nuffink else there – just fields.'

Oh, horror of horrors. All that green and those scary sheep and cows. 'She didn't say anything else about it?'

'Nah. I'd tell you if she did, wouldn't I?' She paused then added, 'Honest.'

Keen to be helpful, Mandy became voluble again about the baby-sitting but couldn't remember, other than vaguely, exactly where that was done or who for, but it was mainly on the Rainby Estate. That was the dreary council estate which had spread relentlessly over the depressing western edges of Birchfield near the Favourite Meats factory, since the first few houses had been put up twenty-five years earlier.

'You told Sergeant Bridgeman there was no boyfriend.'

'Yeh. Right.' Mandy shifted about on her seat.

The Detective Constable let another short silence grow then murmured quietly, 'But there was, wasn't there?'

'No.' She was defensive. 'Not right then, anyway.'

'Had been though. Recently.'

She nodded. 'They broke up, didn't they?' she said. 'He got fed up waiting around for her while she did this baby-sitting and everything and—'

'Did they have a fight?'

'Yeh.' To Carol's amazement the girl began to blush. 'But he wouldn't have done nothing to her. He's a good bloke. They was, well, too different to each other. He's two forms above her and. . . .'

Such a spirited, unsolicited defence. 'And he's your boyfriend now?'

Mandy's eyes widened and the blush became crimson. ' 'Ow d'you know that?'

Oh, such innocence behind the girl's knowing veneer. Carol knew Mandy must see her as being quite ancient and having the sex-appeal of boiled cabbage, not to mention being out-of-it as far as her young world was concerned. She little realized that some things are bloody eternal. Such as a girl pinching her friend's boyfriend. Hadn't it been done to her in Form 5A by that minx in the skimpy shorts?

'Experience,' Carol sighed, feeling about ninety-five and mouldy around the edges. 'Cross about it, was she?'

The girl gazed down at her feet and muttered something.

'Come again?'

'She didn't know.'

'Was she upset about the fight then?'

'First she was. Then she just said, "Sod him! Just you wait, he'll be sorry". She went on about something fab was going to happen and everything was going to change. We was going to be knocked out and he would want her back. But she'd say sod off.'

'Dreamt a lot like that, did she?'

'Nah. Not usually.' To her surprise the girl's clear grey eyes began clouding with tears and she began compulsively tucking invisible strands of hair into her ponytail. 'I thought maybe she'd got a chance to be a model. She was always sending her pictures away and going in for competitions and that.'

'But she didn't have any *extra* money yet? Not that you saw?'

Mandy shook her head and the tears began to spill. 'Here, you don't think nothink's happened to her, do you? She was my best mate and she was a good laugh. . . .'

'No,' said Carol with grammatical truth. 'I don't think nothing's happened to her.'

'My wife used to do watercolours,' said DS Bridgeman, 'so I learned a little bit about the "wet-in-wet" technique and "lost and found edges".'

'Used to? She's given up painting then?'

He grimaced. 'No, just given me up.'

'Oh, sorry.'

He shrugged. 'The CID are the proud holders of numerous world records in the divorce stakes.' He sipped his coffee appreciatively. 'So,' he began, 'we have established that you are *not* Mrs Furness, so who are you?'

'Jenny Warrender, aged 27. House-sitter extraordinary. Self-taught artist and anything else that I think might help me earn a crust.' Hector jumped on to his lap and began kneading his thighs.

'Home address?'

She looked rueful. 'There isn't one now, I'm afraid.' She sighed. 'Negative equity and redundancy struck in awful unison.'

'Oh, tough.'

She nodded. 'We used to live about forty miles away. Little place called Sprecklington.'

'I know it.'

'After we lost our house, renting had gone sky high – so house-sitting seemed a good temporary solution. We get a decent place to live.' She laughed. 'Lots of variety.' Now she'd started talking she didn't seem to be able to stop. 'The heating and lighting bills are someone else's and, meanwhile, Robin goes job-hunting and I do my best to earn a little in various other ways – with the pictures and with the other sort of painting – I sometimes do a bit of decorating for folks while they are away.'

'Good idea,' he nodded, spattering some biscuit crumbs as he spoke and looking embarrassed. He wiped his mouth. 'But I'm surprised you're in an isolated place like this on your own.'

'So am I. It's accidental I assure you.' Hector had transferred his affections to her and she pushed his bottom down to settle him, and began stroking. 'The people at our last sit missed their return flight so my partner, Robin, had to stay over till they got back this morning. He'll be here, God willing, in a couple of hours.' Hector didn't want to be settled and dug in his claws to spite her, then jumped down and stalked off.

'Good. Bit isolated here for a woman on her own.'

He's trying to make up for scaring me to death, thought Jenny, scaring me even more in the process. Nice, though. Plenty of blokes would think she was just being a wimpy woman. So would she have done, once. Before the Mildenbrook business.

She watched as he jotted down the house-sitting agency's details. His face had altered since it became relaxed, letting his rather whimsical personality shine through. He even looked quite handsome. That often happened, Jenny found. How many times had she been taken in by handsome hunks whose divine features became plain and even unpleasant, once she'd realized how thick and totally self-obsessed they were.

He looked up. 'So, how long will the Furnesses be away?'

'Couple of months. Nice long sit. Once Robin's here, we can get settled in.'

'And some painting done?'

'Yes.' She gave him an old-fashioned look. 'But not quite so wet-in-wet.'

He made a guilty face and looked out of the window. 'You could do a picture of that view for the Tate.'

'Only if I painted it purple and yellow, chucked dung at it, and hung it upside down.'

They both laughed.

'So, did Mrs Furness mention anything about Linda coming to clean?'

'Never met her.'

'Oh.' He looked surprised. 'Is that unusual? I don't know the drill for this sort of thing.'

'Well, usually you pop over to meet the prospective clients to see if they like you and if you are happy with their setup and them and their animals.'

'But this time you didn't?'

'Oh yes, we did. But it was just him. She'd had to pop off to get a last-minute jab for their trip. He apologized, but it often happens, although it's usually the man who can't be there.'

'And *he* didn't mention Linda?'

Jenny shook her head. 'No mention of a cleaner at all. Most of the places this size do have one cleaner and some clients keep them on while you're there. Partly to be nice to us. If they are happy with you they want to keep you,' she explained, 'and partly so they don't lose their cleaner. Good ones can be hard to find – and people don't like change. Training in a new one can be a bit of a nuisance. On the other hand, some clients might give the cleaners a couple of weeks off while we're there.'

'Would have thought the Furnesses might have kept them on when it's two whole months?'

'Yes, I suppose so. But it just didn't come up in conversation. We just accept what they want to do.'

'Have you a telephone number where you can contact the Furnesses?'

'No. They're touring.'

'Where?'

'Australia and New Zealand. Mr Furness said they would ring us every week just to check everything is OK.'

'And is it?'

'Oh, yes, fine.' She held up a finger. 'There is a contact in Birmingham.'

'Birmingham?'

'Yes. Mr Furness's brother. Clients are asked to give an emergency contact in case anything goes really wrong – roof falls in, or something like that, and you need help or permission to take action.'

'Oh, right.'

'But he's a bit far away and, anyway, I got the impression he wouldn't know anything about the nitty gritty such as cleaners.'

She sighed. 'Clients do tend to be a bit cavalier on that point. We had one contact who was supposed to help us if we had any problem, but when we bumped into her in the park she calmly told us she was off to the States that weekend – and we still had another ten days' sit to do. As it happened, we did have a crisis and could have done with her help.' She was talking too much. Must be the forced isolation.

'People are unbelievable,' he said feelingly and stood up. 'Mind if I have a quick look around while I'm here?'

'Er. . . .'

'Won't take long.' He moved towards the hall door as he spoke. 'Don't worry, I won't be taking up the floorboards or trashing the cupboards.' He smiled, opened the hall door and stood back to let her through.

Interesting technique, Jenny thought. A polite, easy-going, bulldozer. Did they teach them that in training school?

It was indeed a quick look but whilst it was going on his eyes darted everywhere. A friend who worked for the police once told her how to spot a plain clothes police officer. 'They'll be the ones who enter the room, heads still, but eyes doing a 180 degree sweep – even when it's only the police canteen.'

He was upstairs, reaching for the worn and dented brass doorknob when she remembered that this was the locked room. 'Oh, I forgot to say. That room is locked. Which is a bit strange.' She blushed and felt guilty as though she had deliberately kept something from him, which was silly. She'd just forgotten.

He turned hard and pushed. The door opened instantly.

3

Local history, gardening, photography, crosswords. So far, so average, thought Jenny. After-lunch coffee in hand, she was perusing the first row of the TV room bookshelves. Ah – a touch of am-dram enthusiasm here if she was not very much mistaken. Several biographies of well-known actors sat alongside how-to volumes on theatrical make-up, direction and even, perish the thought, *Putting on a Pantomime*!

But the biggest section on the non-fiction shelf was given over to jewellery from the coffee-table tome, *The Best of Fabergé*, through to smaller books telling you how to make your own. This tied up with what she and Sergeant Bridgeman had come across in the once-locked room: boxes of ear-ring wires, brooch backs, multi-coloured beads and glittering semi-precious stones, all tidily stacked on the shelf over the chest of drawers. 'Findings', these bits and bobs were called, she now learned from one of the paperbacks. Jenny had often fancied having a go at jewellery-making. She must have a peek in Mrs Furness's jewellery basket to see how her efforts turned out.

The phone rang. She started, spilling her coffee on the pale, sage-green carpet. It was Robin.

'They've arrived at Heathrow, sweetie,' he exclaimed chirpily.

'Thank goodness for that.'

'With luck and not too much traffic on the M25 I should be with you by mid-afternoon.'

'Can't wait.'

'You're insatiable.'

'I'm lonely.'

'Me, too.'

No sooner had she replaced the receiver and started off for the kitchen and the carpet wipes when the phone rang again. All or nothing she thought.

It was Mrs Ames, their house-sitting agent, making her usual telephone rounds. 'How's things?'

'Oh, everything's fine. Nice place. Lovely garden.'

'You OK there on your own?'

'Oh yes! No problem,' she lied. Telling Mrs Ames she was scared witless at every little noise would hardly help her image as the imperturbable domestic guardian. Joke was, Aden Bullen had been a silent worker.

'Good, sorry you had a glitch there.'

'That's OK. Robin should be here by this evening.'

They discussed one or two other up-coming bookings and she ended, as usual, with, 'So, no problems, then?'

'No, none.'

No point either in telling her about the attentions of the local fuzz. It was just routine, the sergeant had said. Nothing to do with the house-sit and nothing had come of it. She blushed at the memory of the locked room opening without resistance at Sergeant Bridgeman's touch. The man must have thought her loopy, but he just shrugged and muttered something about ladies having weaker wrists. Her friends said that the police were used to dealing with oddballs – particularly those who thought their neighbours were sending electric currents through the walls and poisoning their cats. With her little locked room she probably appeared a mild case by comparison.

Inside, the room had all been boringly normal. No mangled corpse stretched across the spare bed. No stack of drugs in the bedside cabinet or smoking gun on the dressing-table. It didn't even look untidy or as if it had been 'turned over'. It just seemed like anyone's clean and tidy, slightly musty, little-used, spare bedroom-cum-study.

Later, she'd tried the door again and it had opened easily. She had been so certain it was locked that first time. Were her nerves making her imagine things like, the feeling that there was some-thing odd about the whole house? She stared about her agitatedly. She must get a grip. Then it hit her. There *was* something strange. Not something present: something absent. There were no photographs on show anywhere. No beautiful brides. No bouncing babies. No proud graduates with even prouder parents. Not exactly odd, she finally admitted to herself, but unusual.

The lad could scarcely cross his legs so large were his thigh muscles. DS Bridgeman gazed at them in awe. To have body-built to such an extent by the age of seventeen? Maybe Jamie Brown had started out big and just expanded on that but, Bridgeman suspected, with that sceptical policeman's mind, those chest muscles causing straining to his shirt buttons and biceps and making the lad's sleeves look like tourniquets, had probably had a little outside help. Or rather, inside help. And that brought another thing to mind which certainly sent the boy racing up the suspect stakes. It wasn't only that few women would be able to fight off a boy with such strength and bulk but also that which had helped provide the bulk might make him more likely to attack her: steroid rage.

Bridgeman had to admit that the idea of rage sat oddly on the boy now facing him across the interview-room table. His features were pleasingly regular but unexceptional; his hair fair, crinkly and unremarkable and his complexion fresh and clear, but merely typical of a young skin which has managed to avoid the curse of acne. The smile was something different. It just beamed on and off all the time as he spoke. A lovely, lively, very sincere smile. Extremely fetching. But maybe it didn't mean much?

Something he had learned about smiley people came to him: their smiles were always the same. He had noticed it in photographs of his wife with others. Their smiles varied each time: sometimes half smiles, other times cheeky, lopsided grins, occasionally smirks, and sometimes they showed their teeth in a wide and winning flash. But Hannah's smile, like that of many other smilers, was always wide, winsome – and exactly the same each time. How did they do that? What did it mean? That they turned it on? Practised in front of a mirror? That it was a habit or affliction like a facial tic? He didn't know.

The boy had stopped smiling now, though. Now he'd realized that Linda's absence was looking serious. Indeed, by the increasingly troubled look in his eyes and the catch in his voice as he talked about her it soon became apparent that it was she, not Mandy, who was his love. When pushed, he admitted it.

'I just went with Mandy to make Linda jealous.'

'But wasn't it you who broke off with Linda?'

He shrugged his massive shoulders, 'Oh, yeh. But it was because she just didn't seem to care no more. She always seemed to be thinking of something else when I talked to her.'

'And didn't seem to fancy you any more?' asked DC Raycie quietly.

He blushed, stared at her then said, 'Right. Yeh.'

'So you had an argument?'

'No. Not really. I just told her if she wasn't interested no more there was other girls who would be.'

'Girls like well-built lads?'

'Yeh.'

'And what did she say?'

'Sod off, then.'

The memory of this peremptory dismissal clearly hurt. But, then again, it didn't quite tie up with Mandy's report claiming Linda had said she'd show him. Mandy had also said Linda hadn't known about her and Jamie so how could she have been jealous?

'So, did Linda find out about you and Mandy?'

'Dunno. But she soon would have at school.'

'Mmm,' said DS Bridgeman.

Suddenly the lad banged his huge fist on the table. 'What's happened to her?' he pleaded. 'Where's she gone!'

'Don't know, son. Don't know. Meanwhile, I'd be grateful if you would go through your movements last Thursday afternoon. Just routine you understand.'

Robin was deep in his usual pastime these days – perusing job ads in the newspaper columns and the advertising business magazine, *Campaign*. Once a high-flying account executive for Barklyne and Smarts, the current number one agency, Robin had been a big earner. A combination of an unlucky error handling the important, Beadles Dog Biscuits account which had caused that big spending client to drop the agency and coinciding, as it did, with one of those sudden advertising lows placed Robin right at the top of the list for the chop when the inevitable dead-heading began. Now, even the companies who had previously tried to head-hunt him fought shy. You were only as good as your last campaign and Robin's had been a disaster.

With his Beadles For Bounce campaign he had, it was claimed, made pet owners appear witless pawns and dogs just greedy little sods. Result, nose dive in sales. In his defence he had claimed that the intended subtle humour had somehow become lost in the making. But to no avail. The leper syndrome had come into play. Old colleagues, with whom he had had hilarious brain-storming sessions; with whose help he had excitedly and nervously pitched for accounts and jubilantly celebrated with afterwards, now crossed the street rather than come face to face with him. Who knows, the taint might rub off.

His initial period of despair had recently been replaced by dogged over-optimism. The business was heading for another boom, he'd heard. The big agencies would soon be in desperate need of extra experienced hands and, he told Jenny, he wanted his name to be in their minds when recruitment began. And that meant putting his face about and reminding them of his bonanza successes.

Trouble was, his job-finding efforts tended to dip too deep into what little resources they, and particularly Jenny, were able to drum up. The cost of stationery, postage, photocopying and fares up to town to spy out the land mounted up frighteningly. But she could scarcely discourage him. As he told her endlessly, 'You have to speculate to accumulate'. He had been the big earner before and would be again. Only next time they would handle their resources better.

She looked at him fondly as he polished off his apple pudding. His dogged optimism touched as well as irritated her. It must be hard to maintain sometimes. Robin always relished playing the art critic and had an accurate eye for some things so she showed him her attempt at the big garden view.

He gave it the learned once over, head on one side. 'The slope on the hut roof is up the creek.' Linear perspective was Jenny's *bête noir* and she relied on Robin to keep her straight. 'It should slant down a bit more there.' He held his hand at an angle over the painting.

'Yes, I see. I'll adjust it.' She paused, she hated begging for approval but seemed to need it more these days. 'Apart from that?'

'Hmm,' he pursed his lips. 'Yup, very nice. I like Hector there, sniffing at the rose bed as usual.' He was holding back.

'Too loose for you?'

'No, but a bit indistinct over there, isn't it?' He pointed to one of the far flower beds.

'Oh, but it's meant to be like that. It's aerial perspective. You make things less distinct, the shapes smaller, edges woollier, colours paler – so they appear to be further away.'

'It does that all right. Looks right out of it to me!' he laughed. 'That bit,' – he pointed – 'needs sharpening up.'

He was always so irritatingly sure about everything. She had only begun to feel that his confidence could be misplaced when she had heard him laying down the law about something which she knew for certain he knew nothing about: the sport of boxing. It was partly a male bullshit thing, she knew. But it made her uncertain how much to take his advice when it came to her painting. Some of it was right, she realized, but how much? He was entitled to his taste and opinions if only he didn't treat them as the final word. Himself as the ultimate arbiter. Pity he was her sole critic while work was in progress. Stop being so wet, she told herself. Make your own judgements for goodness' sake!

'Thanks love,' she said and put the picture away.

She *had* been grateful for his confident reassurance that the locked room was of no consequence. The lock-bolt had been stuck and her rattling about had, while not unlocking it, loosened it so that it opened easily later. Nothing the least peculiar about it. The lack of family photographs also failed to impress him. 'Some people do, some people don't, sweetie. I mean, look at us. We don't have images of ourselves leering and grinning from every nook and cranny, do we?'

That was true. 'But it's different if people have family, isn't it? Toddler pics, pony cup pics, daughter getting a degree, son accepting a rugby cup, weddings, christenings?'

'Are we sure they have a family?'

She thought about it for a moment. 'Didn't Furness say something about a daughter or—'

Robin shook his head firmly. 'Don't remember that.'

'So where did I get the idea? Maybe Mrs Ames mentioned it when she gave me the booking. . . ?'

But Robin was back in *Campaign*, deep in his old world.

When the phone rang, Bridgeman and Carol were discussing the DI's refusal to give major status to Linda's disappearance on the grounds that she was a known 'runner'. They had pressed him but been resisted. A feeling was not evidence and resources were too stretched. He had, however, gone as far as authorizing another assistant, DC Stone, to help extend enquiries and also given permission for them to organize a low-key house to house and road check the following day. Bridgeman was parleying with uniform branch about this when Carol picked up the receiver.

'What?' said Bridgeman, when she put it down again and looked over at him.

'Another teenage schoolgirl missing after school.'

'Oh, God.' He chucked down his pen. 'Last seen where?'

'Leaving the school grounds and,' said Carol ominously, 'this one is *not* a known runner.'

'Oh well,' snapped Bridgeman sourly, 'perhaps we might be granted our wonderful major status now. What's her name?' He picked up his pen again.

Carol paused, then said quietly, 'Cynthia Rolls.'

Bridgeman raised his head very slowly and stared at his colleague. She nodded. 'That's right. His daughter.'

'Good God.' He laughed a hollow laugh and shook his head back and forth. 'I don't believe it! I just don't believe it!'

'Divine retribution?'

'You can say that again.'

'I'm off to see him now.'

'Me, too.'

Carol grimaced before murmuring as diplomatically as possible, 'Is that a good idea, d'you think, Sarge?'

'A bloody good idea!' He struck his palm with his fist. 'A bloody good idea. Let's see how damned supercilious he is now – the bastard!'

4

According to his wife, Hannah, the Hayden case had taken over Bridgeman's life. In fact, it had just about ruined it, its effect on him being the catalyst which had finally driven her away. He glared through the windscreen, scarcely noticing the rain lashing against it as Carol drove them to see Rolls.

'I didn't even know he lived around here.'

'Just moved in, apparently,' she muttered, as she screwed up her eyes to better see the space the wipers were fighting to keep clear. The solid blackness of the night which closed down around them in the country lanes didn't help. Fortunately, her concentration was not further disturbed by the sergeant. He was hunched up in the front passenger seat beside her, now morosely silent and deep in his own thoughts.

He'd scarcely been home throughout the case and on the rare occasions he had, he'd been even more distracted and unliveable with, Hannah had claimed. The Hayden case had really got to him. The state of the victims had made him so angry that he had felt a wonderful relief and triumph when he finally nailed the bastard who'd done these things. Or, at least, thought he had, until this man Rolls not only brought all his efforts to naught but did it with such cynicism, such disdain that it turned Bridgeman into the baddie in the process.

'It seems our sergeant has been less than meticulous,' he had murmured in his languid but loaded manner. 'Or maybe' – slight, rueful smile here – 'that's putting it a little too kindly.

Downright careless, or even worse!' he had thundered suddenly. 'I leave you to come to your own conclusions.' They had all of them been wrong, as prosecuting counsel brought out, but the seed had been planted and took root: Bridgeman was corrupt.

All the time Hayden, the blond Adonis, had just stood there looking angelic. His ice-blue eyes registering hurt and bewilderment that anyone should accuse him of such things.

Hannah had understood his anger, even agreed she had known what she was taking on when she married him, but she had found she could no longer live like that, had packed up and left.

'I think this must be it.' Carol slowed down to peer at the wrought-iron gates looming to their left. 'Can you see what it says?'

He squinted out at the dripping name board. Gold letters on green. 'Something Hall . . . Ripton, that's it, Ripton Hall.'

'Bingo.' He made to get out but she stayed him. 'They're expecting us.' She turned left, drove right up to the gates and pushed against them gently. They began to swing back slowly, allowing them access to the long, gravel drive ahead. The rain was easing off now. Carol glanced anxiously at Bridgeman.

'Don't worry,' he said bluntly. 'I shan't kick him in the balls.'

'Oh, good.'

'Or crow over him.'

'Even better.'

To their left they were passing a tennis court; on their right was a large pond aspiring to be a lake. All right for some.

'My own fault. I should never have let it get to me like it did.'

'You're only human.'

'I don't feel it.'

The rain had eased by the time they drew up before what could only be described as a mansion. The door had opened as the security light flashed on and there, sheltered by the Palladian-style portico, stood Rolls.

Bridgeman could scarcely believe it was the same man. He still looked handsome and sleek as a Burmese cat, even in casual clothes. The grey and white-striped sports shirt, grey slacks and charcoal loafers had that sheen of quality about them. But the dark hair flecked with distinguished silver was now dishevelled and the look in those cool eyes distraught. Another thing which startled the sergeant – rocked him almost – Rolls obviously did not recognize him.

'Come in, Officers, come in.' He ushered them quickly through the wide hall and into a large lounge beautifully decorated in creams and pale yellow giving a sunny and expensive effect. He indicated they sit on one of the two long, low settees covered in oyster slub damask. Then, to Bridgeman's added amazement, this silkiest and smoothest of men began pacing the room and babbling about his daughter. 'She's always back by half past five. Always lets us know if she'll be late . . . she's no worry to us. . . . We—'

Bridgeman held up his hand. 'First off, sir. Did she always use the same transport to get home?'

Rolls was startled. 'But I told them. At the police station when I phoned!' His voice was rising accusingly. 'Haven't you been looking for a black Mini!'

'Yes, sir. Of course, sir. A black Mini with silver trim.'

'I would have given her something else. Something bigger, smarter, but that was what she wanted. Small, less conspicuous. . . .'

Bridgeman put his hand up again. 'I've got to take you through this in an organized way, sir. We don't want to miss out anything, do we? Be less than meticulous?' Despite his promises of good behaviour it took effort for the DS to keep the heat and irony out of his voice but Rolls didn't notice.

'Sit down, sir,' Bridgeman said eventually.

The man stared at him and sat abruptly.

Gradually, they managed to slow Rolls's flow to coherence and extracted the information that his seventeen-year-old daughter, Cynthia, was a day girl at Saint Olga's Girls School. Previously, she had been a boarder for two years but they had missed her so much they decided to buy a house nearby rather than move her from where she was happy. They had moved in just three months before when she became a day girl. On days when there was no after-school activities she was home by 5.30 p.m. prompt. There had been no after-school activities that day.

'What are her hobbies and interests, sir?' enquired DC Raycie.

He turned his dazed glance towards her, 'Is that—?'

'Relevant? Yes, sir. It gives us a picture, suggests contacts etc.'

He nodded trance-like. 'Er . . . horse-riding, music – she played a cello in the school orchestra, hockey and painting.'

'All took place at school?'

'Yes.'

'No extra outside lessons – with the cello for example?'

With a teacher who might have raped and murdered her, Bridgeman thought angrily.

'No.' Rolls hesitated pushing his fingers through his rumpled hair. 'At least, I don't think so. Clara – my wife – would know. . . .'

They had already established that Clara was *en route* from London at this very moment and should arrive in about an hour.

'Don't worry, sir, they'll be asking that at the school as well, right now,' said Bridgeman. 'What about friends outside school?'

'None.'

'None at all?'

'No. Not deliberately or anything. Not snobbishness. It's just that there was no need. No occasion. When she was a boarder, everything revolved around the school and, even now, the children of the people we've met all attend either St Olga's or Belvedere.'

Belvedere was the boys' equivalent in privileged education. They were tempted to probe the boy element, but the man was near to tears and, anyway, mothers were better sounding boards on such subjects. Bridgeman reached out and patted the man's arm. 'We get lots of girls going missing sir and they nearly always turn up, I promise you. They're somewhere they've forgotten to tell you about, or you may have forgotten to note.' He couldn't believe he was saying that to this man.

Rolls looked at him properly for the first time. A puzzled expression came into his eyes. 'Do I know you, Officer? You seem familiar.'

Carol tensed and Bridgeman drew a deep breath, 'I was the officer in the Hayden case, sir.'

'Hayden case? Hayden case? I'm sorry. . . .'

'Six months ago. Multiple rape.' He looked away before murmuring, 'A nasty case.'

Rolls went white then exclaimed, 'Oh God! Oh God! No!' and began to cry. Through his sobs he stuttered, 'This must be of great satisfaction to you, Officer.'

'No, sir,' said Bridgeman and, to his own amazement, meant it. 'I promise you, it really isn't.'

'Well, what do you reckon?' Bridgeman asked on their way back to the station.

'I think Miss Cynthia has a boyfriend.'

The sergeant glanced at the girl's photograph and nodded. 'She's certainly old enough and tasty enough.'

'And, despite Dad's fond delusions about her being safe in the bosom of the school, there are always ways and means.'

'Apart from her age and the urges, what have we got to indicate there's a boyfriend?'

'Well, for example, what does she do from four p.m. when classes finish, to five-thirty when she arrives home?'

'You don't buy this gossiping and giggling in the games room?'

'It's too precise, isn't it?' Large drops of rain began to splatter on to the windscreen again. Carol switched on the wipers with a sigh. 'If she was just talking to friends it would be half an hour one day, ten minutes the next, forty the next.'

'Makes sense.'

'This precision suggests a tryst to me.'

'You dear, old-fashioned thing.'

'She meets someone who is only able to sneak off from work, or home, or school, or wherever, right around that time for a set amount of time. Or, maybe she judges that's as much time as she can get away with.'

'But why the secrecy? No reason why she shouldn't have a boyfriend, is there?' He paused. 'Unless, of course, daddy might think he was socially below her.'

'Right, I didn't buy that not snobbishness bit either. Why mention it?' Thunder rumbled in the distance. 'Or maybe the bloke's married, or in a position of trust as regards the girls.'

'A teacher.'

'Could be.'

'Or,' – as the thunder grew louder and nearer and the rain began lashing across Carol's field of vision again and bouncing off the bonnet, Bridgeman raised his voice to say what had been at the back of both their minds, 'or, we have an old-fashioned abduction on our hands. A run of the mill, unimportant, no consequence, rape and murder.'

'Don't get bitter.'

'She was stopped on the road on some pretext. Travelling with such regularity someone could have been watching her and planned the whole thing.'

'We need to find out fast whether she could have had contact with someone outside of school.'

His hands balled into fists, 'And we need to know the where-abouts of Hayden.'

'Watch it. You know what his solicitor will say.'

'What am I supposed to do?' he hissed. 'Ignore the bloody possibility!'

A flash of lightning too close for comfort caused her to jump and respond more loudly than she had intended. 'Hey, I'm on your side!'

'OK. OK. Sorry.'

'In fact, you know very well that this is not his scene at all. A medium-sized not very prosperous country town with some farming and a lot of failing light industry.' She indicated the sad,

41

dilapidated Blessington shelving factory to their left. 'And it couldn't be further from his MO.'

'I know, I know. But the bloody maniac might have changed it – just to bugger us up!'

'You're getting paranoid.'

'Only because they're out to get me.'

'Anyway, he went back to Scotland.'

'Hmph.'

'I have a discreet mate in Grampian. . . .'

'So have I. And I've been in touch.'

Linda and Cynthia made an unlikely duo, thought Carol. The two girls, unknown to each other in reality, she presumed, were now side by side staring from the CID room wall along-side a large incident map adorned with red spots for last sightings, green spots for places frequented and red lines for routes taken.

DC Haldane, the bubbly woman officer who had been out at St Olga's, was giving her interim report, having left a couple of uniformed officers at the school to carry on. So far, she had estab-lished that the only males who visited the school were an art teacher on Tuesday afternoons, a temporary science teacher on Thursdays and Fridays and a football/cricket coach on Wednesdays and Saturdays. The amused, signs-of-the-times, sidelong glances were wiped off the faces when Haldane, with mischievous timing, added casually, 'Oh, and the boys from Belvedere on disco nights and one or two other shared events.'

Her audience groaned as one.

'Oh, blimey,' muttered Bridgeman, that's all we need. A whole bloody boys school.'

'Well, to be honest,' Haldane admitted, 'just the senior boys.'

'How many?' Bridgeman sighed.

'About fifty.'

'And they send along masters, too, to make sure they behave themselves?'

She nodded apologetically. 'Two, at least.'

'Why couldn't she have gone to a convent school?' he groaned.

A mumble of agreement and caustic comments was quickly silenced by Detective Inspector Glass. 'And workmen?' he prompted. He was a precise, needle-sharp, ultra clean and neat man who, to everyone's astonishment, had managed to enforce his pristine standards on the normally sordid CID office seemingly without them even noticing.

'A couple of gardeners three times a week and a middle-aged boiler stroke handyman. Terse old bugger who claims not to be able to tell one girl from another.'

This produced a roar of disbelief. Glass allowed himself a slight smile before holding up his hand, quietening them immediately. 'Not boyfriend material, we gather, but a possible, simmering, sex offender?'

Haldane inclined her head in agreement. 'We're including tactful questions about him in our interviews with the girls.'

'And, as to Cynthia herself?' His very way of saying the girl's name gave it dignity and reflected concern about what had happened to her.

'So far – seems to be on the quiet side. Not flirty, in fact a bit shy with boys, even though they fancy her because she is so pretty. No info about anyone special. The other girls like her. No jealousies or bad feelings mentioned – yet. Oh, and the other girls got the impression that Cynthia's parents were a bit smothering and over-protective. Particularly the father.'

'Ah. Interesting.' Glass paused. 'And after school?'

'If there is nothing on might stay chatting for ten or fifteen minutes. Today, she didn't stay at all.'

That news was greeted with silence.

5

Luke and Jimmy Finch disobeyed parental instructions and strayed from their campsite while supper was being prepared. Not disobedient lads as a rule, they saw no harm in playing in the nearby woods for half an hour. That's what woods were for. Firstly, they climbed some of the elm and beech trees which had been planted around the edges of Stally Woods in an attempt to hide the Douglas Firs – which protesters had dubbed 'those ugly, invaders'.

Then, they went a little further in, their footsteps crunching satisfactorily on the pine needles, cones and small broken branches beneath them, disturbing a silence deeper than they had ever experienced. But they weren't afraid. The powerfully fruity scent from the trees was sweet, the campsite close by and a tasty, fry-up supper in prospect. It was all a bit of an adventure – at the start. Soon, after they had stopped to pick up some particularly attractive cones, they began to realize that they weren't altogether sure which way they had come, indeed which way led out of the forest at all.

Ten-year-old Jimmy, a feisty redhead who had been in the boy scouts for six months before being lured away by the local gang, insisted they must keep heading west where the sun was setting, having decided that west was where their campsite lay. But the path seemed to be dwindling away. In this part of the woods, closely planted firs left little forest floor exposed to daylight, or for man to picnic or bird watch. (Indeed, the forestry company preferred such activities to be confined to the designated recreation areas on the outer rim.) Consequently, few interior minor paths had developed and those there were, tended to peter out to nothing.

The light was starting to fade and the low, dense branches seemed to be deliberately thrusting themselves at the boys, scratching their bare arms and whipping back viciously into their faces. Luke who was only just seven, began to cry. Jimmy began to lose his certainty about going west, partly because in the dying light he was no longer sure where west was. They tried to go back but found the way blocked by even denser and lower branches. Panic stricken, they began to push forward again. At least, they thought it was forward.

That was when Jimmy fell over. As he pushed himself up he noticed that the log which had tripped him felt soft. In fact, not like wood at all. He looked down, then screamed. Even in the creeping darkness he could tell that it was not a log at all. It was a leg. He screamed and screamed and tried to run back the way they had come, fell over again, then just stood there hands to his head, yelling, 'Help! Help!'

Luke was stunned. He stopped crying abruptly and stood trembling and wetting himself. If Jimmy didn't know what to do all was lost. Then, suddenly he was tugging at Jimmy's sweater shouting, 'Shut up! Shut up! Listen, listen, I can hear somebody. And look' – he pointed to the left – 'there's a light.'

By the time the nearest local policeman arrived it was quite dark, and he needed all the torches he and the parents could muster between them just to find his way back to the body. It turned out that there was a fire break running almost parallel with the route Jimmy and Luke had stumbled along.

When the news came through to the Birchfield incident-room, Carol was occupied with a check on raves, or what DI Glass referred to as spaced-out barn dances. This was in case Cynthia had attended a rave and, in the process, forgotten she had a home to return to and a loving, if slightly suffocating, family waiting. It did happen. DS Bridgeman was preparing the house-to-house questionnaire for the following day and keeping in touch with the force 'copter out seeking tell-tale hotspots. All this activity came to a halt when the DCI called them together and announced sombrely, 'Ladies and gents. I'm afraid we have a body.'

Bridgeman and DC Raycie waited impatiently in the circle of police cars huddled by the picnic area on the perimeter of the woods. DI Glass and the police surgeon had been gone for half an hour but, until a fresh route had been cut, they were unable to follow for fear of contaminating the original path still further.

'As if the world and his wife haven't done that already,' Bridgeman complained. 'Running lads, anxious mum and dad, the local plod with his great boots. At least, Glass's person is naturally sterile. Those gleaming shoes wouldn't leave any trace, and debris wouldn't dare attach itself.'

Carol shivered. Glass's squeaky clean, external persona was the object of much humorous comment among his underlings, but she was not in the mood. She stamped her feet and said, 'I just wish they'd hurry up.' A bone-chilling dampness clung in the air and it was still very wet underfoot. She was tired and, in her lightweight grey trouser suit, inadequately clothed for hanging about on the edge of a forest at 2 a.m. Eventually, distant flickers of light grew clearer and the snapping of debris underfoot signalled their approach. They emerged, ghostly in their white, non-contamination suits, incongruously wafting the scent of pine along with them.

'Which girl is it?' Bridgeman shot at Glass immediately.

He gave them a long look and grimaced. 'You're not going to believe this.' He paused and leaned wearily against a car. 'It's a young woman all right but the bugger of it is I don't think it's either of our missing girls.'

'Bloody hell!' exclaimed Carol. She and Bridgeman exchanged meaningful glances. A serial killer?

'I need you both to have a look at her as soon as the path is cut and the floods are on. I know you don't know Cynthia and Linda

46

personally but you are more familiar with their photographs and descriptions. A better light should help. Right now I can't even tell the colour of her hair.'

'Right, guv,' said Bridgeman. 'But what if we can't be reasonably sure?'

'Get some teachers out of bed first, I think. Don't want to upset the parents unnecessarily.'

The girl's body lay half-twisted around a tree trunk and half hidden by the undergrowth arranged around her. Both the missing girls had been wearing jeans and crop tops. This one was naked except for thong-style pants, so clothing was no help, which was probably deliberate. The pants being *in situ* must be a first for such a body, thought Bridgeman, and that has to mean something. Like Linda, the dead girl wore a stud in her belly button. But then, so did dozens of girls these days.

Her eyes were closed so they were of no help yet in identification. The nose, Bridgeman noted, was slightly tip-tilted – like Linda's, but unlike Cynthia's. According to her father, hers was quite straight and strong. As for the hair, that of the girl who lay before them was straight and shoulder-length. Now straggly, strands of it clung to her cheeks and were caught up in the rope which had been tightened so cruelly about her neck. Both Linda and Cynthia had shoulder-length, straight hair but Cynthia's was dark and, in the better light provided by the floods, it became clear that this girl was fair.

'Well, the nose and the hair narrows it,' said Carol. 'It's definitely not Cynthia. Is she wearing a silver ring on her left little finger?' she called out.

The scenes of crime officer shook his head. 'No rings on the left hand. Just a gold ring with a green stone on the right index.'

'I'd like the approximate height as soon as you can manage it,' Bridgeman shouted.

The pathologist looked irritated.

Sod him, thought Bridgeman. We've all got our jobs to do. And a miserable bloody job this is. Poor cow, lying there.

Carol shrugged. 'She looks a bit too tall for Linda. Linda is five-three. This one's nearer five eight if I'm not mistaken, but it's difficult to tell in that twisted position.'

'The bottom will clinch it,' murmured Bridgeman.

But they didn't dare hurry the team to turn her over. They'd never be forgiven if something was missed in the rush. They waited, shivering, for the forensic pathologist, the photographer and the SOCO to give the nod. A wind was getting up causing Carol's teeth to chatter. Silly women and their silly clothes thought Bridgeman. He took off his parka and put it around her. This act of kindness warmed her in more ways than one. She felt almost tearful.

At last, they turned the body on its side. 'Sorry to be a pest,' yelled Bridgeman, 'but could you look closely at the right buttock to see whether there is a butterfly tattoo? It's important we know quickly.' The SOCO put his head as close as he dare and scanned the area with the aid of a hand-held light then shook his head. 'How about the left buttock, in case someone's got it wrong?'

The man repeated the procedure then shook his head again. 'No tattoos. But, of course, there might be something under all this debris.' They waited again until the body had been taped to remove everything adhering including the forest floor detritus. No butterfly.

'Not Linda,' breathed Carol. 'Thank goodness.'

'Right,' said Bridgeman. 'Although I don't know why we should be so relieved. Quite the reverse, actually.' They both knew that unidentified bodies were a nightmare. Nothing slowed up a murder enquiry at the vital time, the beginning, as much as not knowing who the victim was.

The day was clear and bright after the rain. Jenny decided to have another crack at the long garden view, but first to find Hector and feed him. Robin had gone up to London on a job interview so she was alone again. But the sunshine and flowers made her feel glad to be alive and pushed away any remaining thoughts that an ill-intentioned person was about to saunter down their lane and do her wrong. Besides, David had phoned to say he was popping in to do a bit of pruning, so that at least would be company for part of the day. Men did have their uses.

Hector was not to be found in the garden or the ground floor of the house. That meant he was probably snuggled up on the bed in the master bedroom. Jenny wandered up, quite able to ignore the creaking stair. As she expected, the big tabby was curled up into a perfect circle in the middle of the sage-green duvet. He condescended to look up on her approach, doubtless considering that she might come over and fuss him. She did. Hector favoured the rough approach, quite firm massaging behind his ears and over his orange-marked head. Not conducive to the dreamy meditative cat stroking of fiction. Kept thus alert, Jenny ran her eye around the room. With its predominant white, green and gold colour scheme the overall effect was fresh and pleasant, even if the numerous knick-knacks on the dressing-table and the tops of long chests of drawers were too fussy for her taste. She spotted two jewel cases and, to Hector's disgust, left him mid-massage to peek inside.

Disappointingly, the contents were the usual run-of-the mill, comfortably-off lady's trinkets. Strings of baroque pearls; handsome brooches; bold, clip ear-rings for wear with a smart luncheon suit and neat, diamanté pendants to twinkle discreetly from pierced ears with evening wear. The edge of a bright blue scarf was peeping out from one of the drawers below. Jenny slid it open to tuck the scarf back in and there, tumbled among silk scarves of every hue and pattern, were the most weird and wonderful jewellery pieces. She pulled out the drawer and held it before her. 'Come on Hector, food,' she said. 'I will study these at my leisure over coffee.'

Jenny was not in the habit of examining clients' personal belongings, but felt that in this case, given her interest, she wasn't being too nosy. The jewellery designs she picked out and spread before her as she sipped her best Brazilian blend, showed all the expected influences; Arts and Crafts, Art Noveau, Art Deco and modern. But they were executed in a most unusual way. The necklaces, brooches and ear-rings were fashioned from ultra fine silver and gold strands woven into intricate cobwebs, scattered with tiny dots of semi-precious stones. Golden citrine, lustrous green peridot and alexandrite glowed and winked subtly as Jenny turned the pieces over in her hands. Clearly an original artist at work here, she thought. The overall theme was green and gold.

She stopped, surprised, when she came to the most spectacular piece, a spun-gold bib. It appeared to be spiked with tiny emeralds and topaz and at its centre rested a large oblong emerald! Couldn't be! Such a valuable necklace wouldn't be left like that lying casually in an accessible drawer. Come to think of it, if it *was* an emerald, it would be pretty unfair of the Furnesses to leave it there, without even informing their house-sitter. Sitters should be told if high-value items were going to be left in their care. Besides which, if knowledge of them got out as these things tend to do, they would be more vulnerable to burglars who adored such easily transportable items. No, she decided, she must be wrong. Like the rest, the stones had to be semi-precious. She was out of practice, that was it. It had been a long time since that evening class jewellery course.

As she was gently replacing the delicate jewels, Jenny's fingers caught against a stiff oblong card jutting up from underneath the drawer's loose black velvet lining. She pulled it out. A driving licence! How odd. Odder still, she thought, when she saw that it belonged to Mrs Joanna Furness, born 6.9.1944.

Why would it be there – hidden at the bottom of a jewellery drawer? Come to that, wouldn't Mrs Furness need her licence for touring in Australia? Jenny shrugged. Maybe Mrs Furness didn't like driving abroad and left it to her husband. She knew many middle-aged women didn't really enjoy driving at all, or couldn't stand their husbands' criticism when they did, so only drove when they went out alone. But, surely, she would have taken it as a back-up in case her husband became unable to drive for some reason? Then again, maybe Mrs Furness didn't know her licence was there? It could have become accidentally caught up with the loose velvet lining. Maybe there had been a panic looking for it when they were leaving?

If there had, strange that Mr Furness didn't mention it when he rang from the airport before take off. One thing for sure, Jenny could hardly tell him she'd found it when he next made contact. They would wonder what she was doing, poking around in their drawers. Never mind, maybe Mrs Furness had got a replacement.

'Oh well,' she murmured, 'it's their problem, isn't it? I can't worry about everything.'

Hector was otherwise occupied, quietly munching his chicken and rabbit Kattomix and didn't bother to look up.

6

'I only got this because I'm a girl,' complained Carol on learning she was to be assigned to Team B. They were to concentrate on finding Linda and Cynthia, dead or alive, and which had already been dubbed the runaway brats posse. Team A were the murder team; identifying the body and some prime suspects their priorities.

'That's right,' admitted Glass, flicking an invisible speck of dust from his tie. 'It's called effectively utilizing your specialist resources. You have some problem with that?'

She knew better. 'No, sir.'

'You are not only female,' he added, 'you are also a mother of girls, which, in this case is pertinent.'

Well, it was the first time *that* had been cited as an advantage, thought Carol. Most blokes made it plain that she should be at home looking after them thar girls.

'Don't worry. You won't lose out. I'll see you get your share of the action. If not now, later.'

Promises, promises. Did that mean fewer rapes and sexual assaults and more armed robberies and murders? She didn't think so.

Separate, but in tandem, was the expression DI Glass used for the arrangement. Input from the two teams would be kept on separate files so as not to confuse the issue with information overload. But there was also to be a third file collating the two.

The indexer would have to be extra vigilant to make sure that no detail failed to appear on the joint file.

DS Bridgeman became the incident-room office manager.

The Press had got hold of the story faster than Glass would have liked. 'We are going to need them desperately unless we have a rapid breakthrough, and I can't see that happening,' he admitted. 'But it would have been nice to have had a short time window. Just a few more hours to talk to the more obvious potential witnesses before the reporters contaminate them and put ideas into their heads.' He turned to Bridgeman. 'Put on a bit of speed with the house-to-house and vehicle checks near the site, will you? I'll hold the hounds at bay for a couple of hours with a statement and a joint interview.'

'Couple of hours? Can you talk on what we've got for that long?' asked the DS, fearful of how much his DI might give away.

'Oh no,' Glass winked. A most uncharacteristic gesture. 'The first hour they will be sitting waiting for me while I am unavoidably detained on some vital development. I will be most apologetic about that.'

Crafty old bugger, thought Bridgeman.

As HOLMES swung into operation, DS Bridgeman got down to his managerial duties. He also had to keep a policy document going for Glass – the SIO (Senior Investigating Officer). This job, he thought, is acronym and abbreviation crazy. It had always amused him that the acronym for Home Office Large Major Enquiry Scheme was HOLMES – given how Sherlock had always run rings around the police.

In addition to all the extra foot soldiers, they now had a receiver to filter incoming info; statement readers; an action allocator and an admin officer – to check they weren't spending too much. A depressing prospect to Bridgeman. They might all be necessary but the full panoply threw up its own problems such as taking on board seconded officers who were unknown quantities and who might turn out to be less than committed to a crime not on their patch, rather than a small number of hand-picked officers whose strengths and weaknesses he knew.

But, he admitted to himself, there was something else that was bugging him. Meeting Rolls had brought back all the Hayden business and the thought that the bastard was still out there charming some other poor girl. Having got away with it what would be next on the agenda – murder? He wouldn't be surprised. Bridgeman could still see Hayden on that final day, smiling warmly across the courtroom at the jurors, while the women students whose lives he had devastated looked on in numb disbelief. The stunning juxtaposition of the severe blue suit and the almost white, blond hair and fair burnished skin made him seem angelically fair and godlike, but stable and respectable nonetheless. Who had stage-managed that persona, Hayden or Rolls?

He dragged his mind back. It was decision time. The dogged DC Edwards would be put on the scent of the scant clothing and jewellery and also be exhibits officer. DC 'Inspiration' Smith – he of the laterally thinking mind – would check if any of the missing girls thrown up by the Police National Computer matched up to their body.

The cacophony subsided instantly Glass and Bridgeman entered the hastily commandeered police canteen. The air almost vibrated with the expectations of the coralled and restless media. Glass sat down and did a very good imitation of real regret at the delay, citing 'urgent developments' as the cause.

'Have you identified the body, then?' came a sarcastic shout from a dark, chubby man with two days' growth. He wore a multi-pocketed khaki vest, more suitable for a trek up the Limpopo than an early spring day in one of the less posh Home Counties.

Glass shook his head.

'Found the missing girls?' enquired a formidably intense, bespectacled, young woman.

'No, no.' He shook his head again and held up his hand commandingly. 'Look, you'll be best served I think by me going through the matter in sequence.' The TV lights glinted off the edges of his polished spectacles. 'I promise you, I'll give you all I can.'

Bridgeman had expected Press attention, but not this madhouse. The news of one dead girl plus two others reported missing, had brought reporters from far and wide, British and foreign. He knew they had been hoping that, by the time they arrived, there would be three bodies. Much more exciting copy in serial killers. But the media were not only disappointed but also bloody annoyed at being kept waiting.

At least, thought Bridgeman, I was able to get through the most vital house-to-house visits before they arrived. This was partly due, he grinned to himself, to strategically placed road checks resulting in traffic hold-ups which had chiefly delayed the Press, while causing the minimum of inconvenience to the public, most of whom were at work. . . . However, the superintendent who had given him permission didn't think any traffic hold-ups in the least funny. Road checks and the resultant disturbance were not things to be entered into lightly.

Glass had started his morning at the scene, viewing it with benefit of daylight. Then he had gone on to confer with the scientific bods, and finally attended the winding up of the post-mortem. He now informed the hungry throng that on the previous evening at about 6.0 p.m., a girl in her mid-teens (he was sorry they could not be more precise at present) had been found dead in Stally Woods by two young boys. Cause of death appeared to be strangulation. The post-mortem was not yet finished. Approximate time of death was uncertain at present. (In fact, the pathologist suspected that she had been kept in a deep freeze somewhere, so it was *extremely* uncertain.) Neither was it clear, as yet, he told them, whether she had been sexually assaulted. That produced a groan of disbelief. But it was true. There were no obvious signs of forced sexual activity. The audience began to get restless. They

55

already knew most of this and they wanted more. Glass gave it to them.

'I'm sure all of you are anxious to be of as much help as possible with this dreadful case and we, in turn, are desperate for your assistance.' He held up a pack of photocopies which he then gave to the PR woman to hand round. 'I've had these drawings made of the deceased and have included a note of the girl's description. We would be grateful if you would give them maximum publicity.'

'Why a drawing? Why not a photograph?' asked the chubby man. 'Did she have facial injuries?'

Glass took a deep breath. 'No. No, she did not have facial injuries.' Bridgeman shifted in his seat. Was his boss giving too much away? 'But a photograph would not be suitable, I'm afraid. For a start, her eyes were closed and there is the normal discoloration due to the way the body was lying. As you probably know, the blood drains towards the side nearest the ground. . . .' To Bridgeman's surprise, Glass paused suddenly and looked about him, as though unsure of where he was. Those old bugbears of the big enquiry – fatigue and information overload? They could be particularly bad at the start, just as well as when well into an investigation. But he'd never seen Glass falter before. Bridgeman thrust a photograph into his boss's hand.

The DI looked down at it dazedly, then swiftly recovered. 'Oh yes, and another way you can help us gentlemen – and, of course, ladies – is to publish a picture of the girl's ring.' He held the photograph up for the TV cameras which zoomed in on it. 'The victim wore it on her right index finger. It is made of gold metal and is of an unusual design: the three wise monkeys encircling a large green stone.'

'That's not an emerald, is it?' asked the earnest young woman.

'Not sure yet, I'm afraid. I've got a jewellery expert coming in.'

'If it is, it would be worth a mint.'

'Quite.'

'Hear no evil, see no evil, speak no evil,' a TV reporter murmured to camera. 'Was this a gruesome warning? Certainly the tragic victim will be unable to do any of those things any more. Do you know who wore this ring?'

DC Carol Raycie frowned deeply as, yet again, she gazed at the photographs of Linda and Cynthia, pinned up on the incident-room wall.

'Does anything strike you about them?' she asked DC 'Inspiration' Smith.

'Mm. Yeh. Two pretty girls. . . .'

'Oh, please. Not the knee-jerk, male reaction. I'm talking about the poses, the style of the photography, that sort of thing.'

'Huh. Jealousy, jealousy.' He studied the pictures again. 'Well, they look professional and a bit – I dunno.'

'Commercial?'

'Yes . . .' he pondered. 'Sort of, as if they were selling something.'

'Themselves?'

'Could be.'

'Anything else?' She paused. 'There's nothing on the back to say who took them, but I thought they had a similar look, apart from that expression. But I can't quite put my finger on it.'

'Well, the background is white in both, which is fairly usual, I think. And that pose – head to one side and eyes looking up into the corner is one they often ask you to assume—'

'Double spot,' murmured DC 'Doggie' Edwards glancing up from his nearby desk.

'Come again?' said Carol.

He got up and strolled over. 'Double catch light in both eyes.' He pointed to the girls' pupils. 'Shows that whoever took them used a double light set-up.'

'Right.' She took time to assimilate this information before asking, 'Is that unusual?'

'Well, it shows that the pic *was* probably professionally taken in a studio, as you suspected, or by an enthusiastic amateur.

Some of them go for the twin catchlight but others think that's a bit flash, if you'll excuse the pun.'

'I'll excuse anything as long as you keep going!'

'Put it like this. Most portraitists would probably go for a single catchlight.'

'Right. That *is* useful, Doggie. I didn't know you were a snapper.'

He cringed at the expression. 'I do a bit.' He peered closely at Linda and Cynthia again. 'Another thing,' he said, 'I'm pretty certain the same soft box and fill-in light system has been used in both.'

Carol held her breath. She was riveted. 'Does all that jargon mean,' she trusted herself to say eventually, 'that the same person took them?'

He shrugged. 'Wouldn't be surprised,' he said. 'Good chance.'

'Don't go away,' she cried, as he tried to return to his desk and pile of exhibits, 'I need you, you lovely man.'

DS Bridgeman interrupted. 'You're wanted in the front office, Carol. Mr and Mrs Rolls have arrived.'

They both started forward as Carol entered the interview-room.

'Any news?' asked Rolls anxiously.

Carol shook her head. 'Sorry.'

The man may have looked more haggard about the eyes this time, but the rest of his appearance was back to normal, just as she remembered it from the Hayden case. Obviously he had come straight from his work: elegant, dark, pin-stripe suit, sparkling white shirt with an ever so subtle silky stripe, dark-red tie with a hint of silver sheen in its spots echoing the streaks in his hair. The whole effect was conservative but with a dash, a flourish, and very expensive, as befitted a top barrister. Carol had to admit the man was handsome – if you liked the suave, sophisticated look. But she was unable to dissociate it from what she had seen him do to Bridgeman. And she liked Bridgeman, a lot. This time, of course, Rolls's manner was different; concerned, helpful, polite. She thanked them for coming in.

'Anything to help find Cynthia,' the man responded. 'We understand your problems, being so busy.'

Oh, really, thought Carol. That's nice.

'This is my wife, Clara.'

Clara Rolls was a fashionably slender woman with a straight, swinging blonde bob and curious amber-flecked eyes. She was turned out in a suitably sober black, designer label, pants suit and chunky gold jewellery and she wrung her hands continually. 'What can we do? It's driving me mad wondering what we can do. We can't bear the thought that she might. . . .'

Carol held up her hand. 'As I told you on the phone, any information you can give us about Cynthia is the way you can help.' She indicated the chairs for them to sit down.

'Yes, yes. We've been thinking. Racking our brains.'

They told her about Cynthia. Her likes, dislikes; her habits, friends, or lack of them as yet, locally, and every physical detail they could remember.

'We've brought more photographs as you asked.' Mrs Rolls produced an envelope and feverishly began spreading them on the table. 'Here's one with her pony; this is a family group; there's one of her at her last birthday party.'

'These should be a great help,' Carol assured her. 'It's useful to have several different views of a person. Just one photograph can be misleading.'

'Sorry we don't have any more close-ups like the one we gave you originally. Recent ones, anyway.'

'Oh, that's all right. That's a very good one as it happens. Who took it, by the way?'

The woman hesitated and frowned. 'I'm not sure . . . oh yes, I remember now. Cynthia brought it home from school. Said it had been done in a photography class.'

'Oh, right,' said Carol. 'A very nice picture. Could grace a model's portfolio. So many girls want to do that these days.'

She said it as casually as possible but felt it sounded clumsy. She could see Rolls's antennae go up. 'What are you insinuating, officer?' There was some of the snap of the deadly cross-examiner in his tone, such as she had heard him directing at Bridgeman when accusing him of doctoring the evidence against that animal, Hayden.

'Insinuating, sir?' Carol replied carefully.

'Suggesting that Cynthia would like to be a model?' He stood up.

'Did I, sir?'

'Oh come on. . . .' The arrogant, bullying barrister quickly surfaced. 'First, it's "where did the photo come from"? Then—'

Carol shot him a glance so icy and full of such unblinkered hatred that, to her surprise, it stopped him in his tracks. He stared at her for several seconds, then whispered, 'You've checked on local sex offenders?'

'Of course, we have them in mind,' snapped Carol. 'But we must be careful that we are not accused of undue harassment. I'm sure you would be the first to stand up for their rights.' She paused. 'Sir.'

Rolls sat down and put his head in his hands.

She knew she shouldn't have said that but couldn't stop herself. She'd seen too many vile rapists got off by men like Rolls. The lowness of the conviction rate made her sick. Well, his chickens had come home to roost now.

Clara stared from one to the other. 'What are you two talking about? Who? What's going on?'

'Now, family and friends,' broke in Carol, in a back-to-business manner. 'More about them. Are you sure, absolutely sure, she could not have run off to see anyone?'

'But, why should she?' he asked, plaintively.

'Oh, you never know, honestly,' said Carol. 'Girls of that age can suddenly take umbrage at something said and run off to lick their wounds. Often with some favourite aunt or best friend. It does happen, believe me, and—'

'Well, at first I did think she might have gone to see her father,' whispered Clara, screwing the damp handkerchief she held in her hands even harder. 'But he's not seen her.'

For a moment Carol was robbed of speech, then managed an

incredulous, 'Her *father*?' She glanced, bewildered, from one to the other.

Finally, Rolls shrugged and admitted, 'Cynthia's my step-daughter.' He paused; then had the grace to look slightly abashed. 'I'm sorry, I thought you knew.'

Why would I? Carol thought. The man had reported his 'daughter' missing and never had mentioned that he was not her real father. Surely, Rolls would know the significance of this to the enquiry? Wait till Bridgeman heard *this*. Husbands might be prime suspects when it came to murders of their wives, but they were as nothing to stepfathers in filling the bill when it came to young girls.

7

Jenny and David both spoke at once.

'May I wash my hands. . . .'

'Please wash your hands. . . .'

They stopped, looked at each other and laughed, Jenny nervously.

The light had been poor in the garden so she had gone inside to paint a kitchen still-life. What Robin called 'the Heather Laxton school of bottled-cherry daubs'. Heather Laxton painted sumptuous concoctions of fruit, flowers, kitchen paraphernalia and draped white cloths. Jenny thought them exquisite despite preferring still-lifes in which the objects had a sensible reason for being plonked altogether. 'Happened upon' was the effect she strived for. On this occasion, she had gathered several pears, a green and gold casserole, a frosted green brandy bottle, a kitchen knife and a recipe book opened up at 'Brandied Pears'.

David glanced over at her painting. 'That looks wonderful.'

'Oh, it's not finished yet.'

'Well, already it looks scrumptious,' he laughed and added sincerely, 'I wish I could do something like that.' Today he was wearing a very crisp, khaki, short-sleeved shirt which set off his lightly tanned skin and brown eyes. His unruly curls had been tamed by a black leather thong which drew them back into a neat pony tail. Less the wild boy Dickon, more nature man, she thought.

Jenny was used to people wishing they could paint like her

and had a stock response. 'Oh, everyone is creative you know. Mostly it's just practice.'

She handed him the towel to dry his hands and suddenly their proximity made her feel self-conscious and very vulnerable.

It wasn't as if she was still doubtful about his credentials: she had already checked up on him by popping into the small market garden from which he operated – on the pretext of finding some large planters for a painting. There he'd been out back watering some azaleas and she'd immediately felt foolish and left quickly in case he spotted her. She felt even sillier when she thought of all the gardeners who had come and gone at other properties without them really knowing who they were. So, now at least she knew David was the man he said he was and that he had something to lose. She had established that. But then, what did that mean? Who could have been more bona fide than Aden Bullen, her brother's best friend?

David seemed to sense her unease at their closeness and moved away towards the table. 'Oh, come on, I'm sure talent must come into it.'

She lifted the coffee pot from the top of the Aga. 'Well, yes,' she conceded, 'I suppose you do have to have a bit of flair.' He was standing by the table waiting to be asked. 'Do sit down,' she said, indicating the chair. 'Like a lot of things, what is most important is persistence and application.'

'You sound like a teacher.'

Just what she'd been thinking. She laughed out loud. 'Well, I am as a matter of fact. I do take evening classes.'

'There you are. I could tell you knew your stuff!'

'Bit of a swizz, really. I'm not art-trained – just good at certain types of picture.'

'But how do you manage to keep up your classes when you're house-sitting?'

'With great difficulty,' she smiled. 'No, seriously, I've been lucky this term. The previous house was for six weeks and was near our caravan which is only twenty miles west of Louden – where I hold my classes. This is an even longer sit and, as it's twenty-five miles north-east of Louden and both sits were early bookings, I knew I could commit for the whole term – for which I was very grateful!'

'Where, exactly, in Louden?'

'Perivales School.'

'Maybe I should join your class,' he said, half-jokingly.

'All are welcome,' Jenny murmured coolly, and began to pour his coffee.

He breathed in the aroma. 'Ah ... here we are. I've been looking forward to this. I've been telling everybody you're the coffee queen of Birchfield.'

They both laughed. Who, wondered Jenny, was 'everybody'?

Jenny was relaxing now, amused by David's tales of the vagaries of market gardening – but making sure the panic button in the hall remained within her sight.

In exchange, she told him about London's volatile property market. It was a place he knew little about, he declared, having spent most of his life on a Hertfordshire farm. 'I know more about Kathmandu,' he laughed.

'Really!' exclaimed Jenny. 'You've been there!' Somehow she hadn't seen him as a fellow gap-year, back-packer. She grinned at him. 'Which road did *you* take – trekking, or lying about in friendly houses, doing dope?'

He gave her a sideways glance. 'A good farmer's lad like me – trekking, of course.'

The wonders of Nepal led on to his experiences in Oz which, in turn, led on naturally to the Furnesses' current expedition.

'I've not actually met Mrs Furness yet,' Jenny admitted.

He looked surprised. 'You wouldn't have, would you? She left, surely?'

Jenny was startled. 'Left?' she said foolishly. 'What d'you mean, left?'

'Just left,' he repeated. 'You know, as in "gone away", "departed", "split".' He sipped his fresh cup of coffee slowly then murmured, 'Greener pastures, Furness said.'

64

She didn't know why she felt stunned. 'When was this?'

He shrugged. 'Oh, I don't know exactly. I just asked after her one day – said I hadn't seen her for a while – you know, the way you do. And he said she'd gone. Just like that. I didn't like to pry any further in case it upset him.'

'But . . . but,' Jenny burbled.

'You look shocked. Is it a problem?'

'Oh, no,' she shook her head, 'of course not. It's just that he said she was not able to meet me because she was up in town, having jabs.'

'Oh well. I expect it's someone new and maybe he didn't want to explain. Didn't think it important.'

'Yes,' said Jenny, 'I suppose that's it.' But she wasn't convinced.

'Nothing unusual, these days, is it?'

'No. Of course, you're right.'

'You know, sometimes I just don't understand you,' Robin complained. 'One minute you're worrying that there are no family photographs around . . .'

'I wasn't worrying, I just thought it was curious!'

'. . . then,' he continued determinedly, 'as soon as you are provided with a reasonable explanation – the family have split – you start worrying about that! What is it about this house and these people?'

They had been having a row ever since Jenny had told him she was thinking of approaching a gallery to sell her pictures as well as trying to hold a local exhibition of her paintings.

'Are you sure you're ready, love?' Robin had murmured solicitously. Always the concerned partner but never very supportive, she was beginning to notice. He acted as if it were vanity which was driving her to do these things when, in reality, it was a desperation for funds. He quickly pointed out how much it would cost to frame the pictures and hire a hall.

'I doubt if the scout hut will cost a king's ransom,' she had snapped back. 'In fact, a lot less than a day in London having boozy lunches on the pretext of keeping up with advertising business.'

'Ah, so *that's* what's getting to you,' he had said, sitting back with a certain smug satisfaction. 'Now, I understand.'

'No you don't! I'm only trying to make us a small crust!'

'Huh. Small is right. Listen, lovey, my seeking work might cost us a little but when I get it, and I will, the rewards will be much greater.'

'While mine will always be peanuts!' she had yelled.

'I didn't say that!'

'Not bloody much!'

By then her head was splitting. Robin had forgotten to buy the aspirin so she went to look in the bathroom cabinet to see if there was anything there which might help. Their clients were hypochondriacs, she soon decided, as she ploughed her way through cough mixtures, indigestion tablets and even Mrs Furness's prescription medicines: Temazepam and two pill strips, one of Modisal and the other, Atenolol. She knew Atenolol was for blood pressure because her father had been taking them.

'They're not the sort of thing you'd leave behind!' she had insisted to Robin. He promptly became irritated again by her strained tone and told her she was becoming neurotic.

'The licence was hidden in the drawer,' he reiterated wearily. 'She didn't know it was there.'

'And the pills?'

'She forgot them.'

'You don't forget medicine like that!'

'She could have been taken off them and put on something else,' he argued. He did have a point there but she wasn't going to admit it. 'We all keep out-of-date medicines in our cupboards, don't we, sweetie?'

Jenny said nothing.

'In any event,' he said more gently, in case she balked at getting dinner, 'we don't know if she left in a hurry, do we, love?' He laughed. 'What are you thinking? That he's murdered her and buried her under the patio?'

'I don't know.'

'Well, *I* do.'

That was the trouble, he always did. It was down to his safe and secure background she supposed – the youngest and most gifted son of an academic family. Oddly, though, his father, Henry, a professor of mathematics, was quite the opposite, an amiable old boy, always interested in your point of view. Maybe he didn't feel the need to prove himself.

At first, Jenny had found Robin's certainty very attractive, coming as she did from a family of insecure people, never quite sure what to do about anything, or of their place in the world. He had pursued her from the first time he saw her at the *Movement in Media* lecture at university. She had been flattered that such a popular, charismatic and astute person had not only noticed her, but had found her problems worthy of his consideration. He had helped her make decisions about her future. But now, she was not quite sure they had been the right ones. He always seemed to be telling her to hold back; that the things she planned would not work; she was not quite ready.

She hadn't been the only one beguiled by his certainties. Others, including his colleagues, not only believed in them but acted on his advice, just as she had done. They had all been greatly shocked when he made his big mistake at work. But, by then, she hadn't. Indeed, that had been the very moment she had begun to have deeper doubts about his judgement and to suspect that it might be no better than hers. Could even be worse, sometimes.

Guiltily, she had realized that she had begun to feel more confident when he was not there, dealt with people quite well despite her allotted role as a social misfit who needed his help. He was only human, she realized, fallible like the rest of them and it was their fault for listening and leaning on him.

But, she conceded when she had calmed down, he was probably right about Mrs Furness. It made sense. A mislaid driving licence and pills replaced by other pills. Either that – or Mrs Furness had been in such a hurry when she left, she had forgotten both.

8

Bridgeman paused for a moment to look at his front garden. Remnants of last year's bulbs were trying to struggle through the weeds. Just like me, he thought, it's in need of some urgent attention. The clouds were lowering but the fresh, early morning air was sweet even to his jaded spirit. It still pleased him that Hannah had discovered this weathered brick and flint farm cottage on the eastern edge of the little village of Hartmeet and only two miles east of Birchfield.

The western side of Birchfield (once a thriving market town now a hotchpotch of everything) might be industrial and depressed but Hartmeet was no such thing. It had leafy lanes, a post office-cum-village store and even a thatched pub which had not been interfered with by brewers because it had refused to be tied to any of them. He drove through the deserted High Street towards the Headington–Louden road and out the other side. To his left, golden-brown Jersey cows back from milking came wandering down a lane towards him, but the leaders were already turning off into a still dewy field to resume their eternal munching. To his right, a field of still green young wheat. Real farm country. Rural but not twee was what he liked about it, he decided. No golf courses or commuter mansions and neither flat nor inordinately hilly. A reasonable kind of place, with currently unreasonable goings-on.

He crossed the Headington–Louden road and continued on to the Stally Woods. Before he got bogged down in the office he wanted another glimpse of the crime scene so, despite a very late night following the Press conference, he'd dragged himself out of bed at dawn. The rain forecast ensured that he wasn't the only one at the scene – which was a disappointment. A posse of sweating young policemen in protective white clothing already had their backs bent as they cleared what ground vegetation there was within the area marked off by day-glo tape. They were stripping it to ground level for packing and labelling before sending it off to the lab along with soil samples. He nodded to the sergeant in charge then stood back trying to blank out the activity and take in the scene before it disappeared as it was fast doing. The low grey clouds were darker now and hung threateningly, preventing much light illuminating the area. The dampness in the air carried the sweetness of cut greenery and mixed with the pine scent to form a potent fragrance.

His efforts hadn't told him much, he decided as he made his way the twelve miles back to Birchfield. So far, their road checks had brought no eureka results either but Bridgeman felt had been worthwhile anyway. A Mrs Hanbury, on a school run to pick up her grandchild, had seen a dark-haired girl in a dark-coloured Mini, driving north towards Birchfield. She remembered her because she'd been angry that the car was being driven so fast in a built-up area and when schoolchildren would be about. They'd showed the woman Cynthia's photograph but she couldn't be sure. 'My eyes,' she had begun to say to the young PC, then pulled herself up and said, 'She went so fast. I didn't have time.' Mrs Hanbury was on her way in to give a statement. If it had been Cynthia she had been driving from the direction of the school – and her house.

They had had less luck with woodside checks, partly hampered by the fact that they had no idea when the victim might have been brought there and whether she would have been dead or alive although they were pretty certain it was the former.

'Maybe, we'll have better luck around nightfall, when the snogging couples emerge,' he said to Glass.

*

'We don't hold photography classes,' said Mrs Springer firmly. The manner was professionally friendly but businesslike.

Headmistresses have certainly changed since my day, thought Carol. This one looked like a blend of something important in the City and one of those rather too well-made-up cosmetic sales ladies from one of the better department stores. The pinky-beige of her crisp, designer suit was picked up by her pinky-beige nail varnish. A creamy, baroque pearl choker and matching ear-rings completed the picture. The detective constable always felt a world away from such women. Why did they spend so much time and energy on their appearance when the end result was so coldly artificial and unappealing? Carol suspected that the distaste was mutual. She had little doubt that Mrs Springer frowned upon her very plain, plain clothes and scrubbed skin and was probably murmuring to herself about 'lack of personal pride' and 'not making an effort'.

'Could any of the girls be doing photography off their own bat?' she enquired politely.

'No.' The tone was unequivocal. 'I'm afraid not. I've asked my staff and they confirm my own impression. There is no photography apart from the usual happy snaps on sports days, family visits and suchlike. As you point out,' she picked up Cynthia's photograph and studied it, 'this is a professional portrait. Although' – she paused to purse her well-painted lips – 'I have to say this is *not* a Cynthia that I recognize.'

'Why is that?'

'Well, it's too knowing and,' she hesitated, then added with some distaste, 'it's also a little provocative, wouldn't you say?'

Carol nodded and thought, she's making it sound as though that's my fault! 'Yes. I suppose I can see what you mean.'

'The Cynthia *we* know is rather on the shy side.'

So would I be with this headmistress, Carol thought. Steel glinted through the woman's calculatingly 'relaxed' attitude.

'May I chat with the girls to see if they can help here?'

'We've done that already, Officer.' She shook her head regretfully. 'None of them has any idea. None of them had seen the picture before.'

Well, that was one avenue firmly blocked off. She could have insisted, but Carol's instinct told her to hold back at this point. Something more urgent would strengthen her hand and give her more reason to talk to the girls in depth. No sense in making an enemy of the woman now.

Linda's mum was much more forthcoming. Desperately eager to help in fact, but unfortunately a little woolly on the details. 'It was that camera shop on the High Street, I think.'

'Which one? There are two.'

'I'm not sure. I expect she said, but I've forgotten.'

'You didn't go with her?'

'No. I was working.'

'But you must have paid for it? Maybe you have a bill somewhere?'

'No, no, I didn't.' She looked down and began to blush. 'The man took them for free.'

There was a short and pregnant silence before Carol could trust herself to say calmly, 'Why would he do that Mrs Blackstone?'

She cleared her throat. 'He needed the practice, that's what he told Linda. . . . He wanted to do more portrait photographs. She began to falter and twist her hands together as the lameness of what she was saying struck home. 'So,' she whispered, 'he was practising on the school kids.'

Carol struggled to keep the incredulity out of her voice as she said, 'Right. Yes. Understandable, I suppose.' Poor woman looked thinner than ever and about to fall to pieces completely. Who was she to push her over the edge?

The results of the house-to-house were also proving disappointing, but Bridgeman was not totally despondent. Sometimes their questions took time to seep into the interviewee's subconscious. After the grey matter had been prodded and stirred by police a sliver of memory or tiny mental snapshot floating on the edge of their mind sometimes began to emerge and, with luck, sharpen and come into focus. The only risk then was whether the person might dismiss the blossoming recollection as too unimportant to bother the police about. Post-questionnaire gossips with neighbours could also tease out images lurking in the backs of minds. He stacked the replies, ready for computer input. Anyway, not all the results were in yet.

Carol stopped by the desk. 'This photography thing,' she said, 'you don't think I'm wasting my time? Going off at too much of a tangent.'

'Have you got anything else?'

'No, not yet. Not really.'

'Run with it, then. I think it sounds interesting.'

'I still have a couple of Linda's baby-sitting parents to interview and Berry Hill House where you went to re-check but the owner there is still uncontactable.'

'Get Edwards to put someone else on the baby-sitting parents. As for Berry Hill House, the owner had left before either girl went missing, so I don't think there'll be much joy there anyway. We'll pop back when we have a spare bod, or maybe I'll go myself later.'

The frontage and decor of POP-IN-PICS belonged to the blocks of primary-colours school of shop-fitting. A fairly recent addition to the Henningford Road shopping precinct, it offered developing and printing on the premises and self-service photocopying in black and white or colour. The shop also sold films, picture frames, photo albums and disposable cameras, but there was no offer of the services of a professional photographer. Not a promising start, but then, Carol reminded herself, Linda had told her mum that the man who took her portrait was only practising – and hoping to gain enough expertise to make a business of it – so her quarry could still be a male member of staff at POP-IN-PICS.

In the event, it transpired that the two young sales persons present were both female. One gentleman was normally there, the elder of the two informed her; Mr Franks, the owner. But he was in London and would not be back for a couple of days. She had no idea exactly where her boss had gone, or whether he did any portraiture. In fact, she didn't seem to know very much about anything. Yes, Joe did 'take a few pictures' but she had no idea what kind and had never seen any of them. Neither had the younger woman. 'We're both new, you see.' Carol took Mr Franks' home address and continued on her way.

CARDINGTON CAMERAS was more of a straightforward, old-fashioned, camera shop with a matching, elderly owner, struggling to keep up with the flash new boys. Selling cameras was clearly his principal business and expertise his main asset. The cramped shop at the less-frequented end of the High Street was packed with stock and, though little attempt had been made to display it in any artistic fashion, each piece of merchandise had its own neatly written card, noting its technical data, current condition and price.

While she was waiting until Mr Cardington had finished enlightening a customer as to the intricacies of an elderly Leica, Carol busied herself studying the ads in a glass-fronted notice-board by the door. This was more like it: several wedding, special occasion, and portrait photographers extolling their own virtues and declaring that only they could capture the magic of your special moments or, as one put it, 'immortalize life's unrepeatable landmarks'.

Mr Cardington, seventy if he was a day, and frail to match, did not present a picture of a likely and possibly suspect snapper of young girls. But you never could tell.

'Oh, I've given up all that sort of thing,' he assured her, when she finally got to speak to him. He was talking about serious photography. 'Take a few of the grandchildren, that's about all.' Won't be doing that much longer either, thought Carol, judging by his wheezing chest and over-high colour.

He perused the photographs of Linda and Cynthia. 'Hmph.

Double catchlights. Could be Jake Runsmith, he goes for the flashy look – mostly glamour, though, I hear.'

This snobbery about how you lit the eyes in a portrait amused Carol, but she tried to keep the smile off her face as she asked, 'Anyone else you can think of?'

He shook his head. 'No. . . .'

She took Mr Runsmith's details and was about to leave when the old boy murmured, 'Of course, where you should go, my dear, are these photography clubs. You'll find all that over-lit sort of nonsense goes on there.'

Of course! Why hadn't she thought of that! She took details of the two nearest camera clubs and sighed. This thing was spreading ever outwards and, if it turned out to be just a red herring, she'd feel pretty silly. Still, that was the nature of the game. Wasn't it?

Jenny felt more alive than she had for ages. She hadn't realized how much she missed London and revelled in the life and colour she was now witnessing from the top deck of a bus as it made its way down Bond Street towards Piccadilly. Her destination was Thatchers Art Gallery, just off Cork Street. She'd brought only two of her paintings which, thankfully, were small, and a portfolio of photographs – prints and slides – of a dozen more. Gazing at the passing scene helped quell the butterflies threatening to take flight in her stomach.

It helped that the early spring day shone brightly making pedestrians look cheerful and encouraging the more headstrong to throw off grey winter wear and blossom into thinner, more colourful clothing, which they'd probably regret later when the sun went back in again. She noticed that even the bus conductor was affected by the atmosphere, exchanging cheerful repartee with any willing passenger and going out of his way to be ultra-helpful to tourists whose polyglot nature added to the colourful interest.

Jenny's attention was drawn back to the passing scene below. A group of jolly Japanese had gathered around an extravagant display of yellow and white Easter bonnets in Fenwicks' window. They were pointing and laughing, and Jenny, too, smiled at the idea of any of these little oriental ladies being topped off by one of those gigantic confections.

Further down Bond Street, she spied two very elegant ladies-who-lunch emerging from Aspreys carrying their spoils in elegant mini carrier bags. She couldn't imagine a more soul-destroying life than theirs but had to admire their style. Both wore soft suits, one in black with exquisitely draped folds dipping across the front of the jacket, and the other a cardigan style in a pale greeny-purple, the like of which even the colour-minded Jenny had not seen before. Obviously quite the latest shade. It never ceased to amaze her how strange new colours were 'invented' every season, and suddenly made everything else look old hat.

Her eye was caught by a man hurrying northwards. She frowned. He seemed vaguely familiar. Yes, she was sure she knew him. But, from where? She strained forward to follow him as he turned into Grafton Street. Then it hit her. Good Lord! It looked like Mr Furness! No, she must be mistaken. It couldn't be. He was in Australia, for heaven's sake! Why would he pretend to be several thousand miles away when he was in London all the time? No, she had to be wrong. It *was* just someone who looked like him. He was out of sight now and she hadn't seen him properly, anyway. Besides, she'd only met Mr Furness once and then briefly, and he had been wearing casual clothes. This man was suited and smart.

But she couldn't get the sight of Mr Furness's *doppelgänger* out of her mind and, for some reason, it tied in with her image of the locked room. Her mind kept shooting back there. It *had* been locked, she *knew* it had. But how could that be? How could it have become *unlocked* when there was no one in the house but herself? Was she going mad? No, no, I'm *not!* she insisted to herself. She got up and lurched her way along the gangway hoping to get to the stairs before the bus braked and threw her off balance completely.

A woman sitting next to the aisle looked startled at the sight of her and Jenny realized it must be her vehement expression. She softened her look but not her sudden resolve. Something *had* gone on in that house: she *knew* it. It had a secret to tell and that secret concerned Mrs Furness and her whereabouts. All she needed was more proof and, by golly, she was going to get it, whatever the cost. Then she would go to the police.

The gallery owner proved distracted and not altogether interested, although he did hit on one of her house interiors and asked if she could produce more like that. If she could he would consider hanging one or two. Always they wanted more of the same – a specific style – was this a disease of the age? But she needed the money and said she would certainly try.

As soon as Jenny arrived back at Berry Hill House, she dumped her things and, giving short shrift to the miaowing Hector, marched straight to the once-locked room where, in a kind of frenzy, she began opening the drawers, searching. Whatever Robin said, she knew she was right. Something had happened to Mrs Furness!

She discovered all the paraphernalia one might keep in a spare room – the overspill from the rest of the house: odd bric-a-brac, notebooks, board games, some more jewellery – this time of a different style, stationery, documents, bills and . . . her heart stopped – a passport. Suddenly she felt frightened and looked about her as if someone might be watching. With trembling hands she opened the maroon booklet and turned to the back inside cover. A handsome, middle-aged woman stared up at her. Beside her photograph, the name: FURNESS, Georgina. And the passport was in date.

9

Tumbling waves, rushing rivers, reflective pools, glistening raindrops and sparkling showers issuing from garden sprinklers – the whole gamut of the world of water was depicted in the pictures ranged around the classroom walls.

'Our latest challenge,' confided Charles Arrow, the club secretary. 'Depict the world of water in its many forms.'

'Impressive,' murmured Carol. She had become a captive audience to this large, pompous and ungainly man with bad breath who was acting as though she was either a candidate for membership or a reporter from the local rag.

The membership of Birchfield Photographic Society was mostly male, Carol noticed, and ranged from the irredeemable anorak to the spoiled young brat with every expensive photographic gadget known to man. Not that it appeared she would get the chance to speak to any of them. On and on, droned Arrow, about the difficulties of keeping a photographic club going these days.

'These days,' Charles explained with some bitterness, 'everyone thinks they can take pictures and don't *need* club support and expertise.' He also objected to the fact that these days good results were so much easier to obtain what with sunset filters and digital manipulation. 'Call me a purist if you like but, if you ask me, it's nothing short of cheating.'

She had partly brought this rabbit-and-stoat stance on herself, she realized. Her low-key, imprecise approach had been designed to prevent panic signals going out. 'I would like to learn about lighting,' she reminded him, when he paused for breath, 'from any portraitists or glamour enthusiasts in the group.'

At the mention of glamour he stiffened.

'We don't encourage *anything* that could be considered pornographic,' he assured her righteously.

'I was thinking of something more on the artistic side,' said Carol.

'Oh well, yes,' he nodded. 'Some of us do a bit of that now and then. But we won't have any of those hard-faced models. Nothing nasty.'

She couldn't help herself. 'I'd imagine you go more for the pure and innocent look?' She'd meant to be tongue in cheek but he nodded agreement.

'Exactly, exactly.'

She wondered how the scattering of female members felt about these 'artistic' evenings. That woman checking through the challenge forms for instance? A dark symphony with her closely cropped black hair, black ski pants and tight-fitting top which revealed a belly button thick with silver studs and rings.

'That's Kathy,' he offered, 'she's into sports photography. Wants to be a professional.'

Clearly he thought the notion bizarre. But now he'd got the idea that Carol wanted to know about the women members. 'We have four lady members,' he explained, as though addressing a public meeting. 'There's Heather.' He pointed to a plump, forty-something woman wearing a loose, printed skirt and floppy top. 'She does child photography and,' he chuckled indulgently, 'she is, I must say, managing to pull quite a few commissions. Not that it's something I'd like to go in for. But then, women have much more patience with children, don't you think?' Actually, Carol didn't. Her partner, Eddie, had been much more tolerant of the girls than she, but now she just nodded. 'Then there's Marian – but she's not here tonight. She's such a busy lady.'

'Right,' murmured Carol, wondering desperately how to lead

him off these listings and on to double spotlights and softboxes without alerting him. She must be losing her touch – or maybe she was just tired. Oh, what the hell, she might as well just plunge stright in, he'd never notice.

His voice was droning on and on. 'Of course, Marian is head-mistress of St Olga's,' he confided proudly. 'So, as you can imagine, she has her work cut out.'

Suddenly the man had her full attention.

'Really?' she asked eagerly, then stopped herself and with suitably polite interest enquired, 'And does she specialize in anything?' At that very moment Charles Arrow's attention was at last diverted. The judging was about to begin. Carol became invisible. Damn.

But what a turn up! Our haughty headmistress, a camera buff who attended meetings at the local comprehensive school? No doubt about it, this case was throwing up some weird bedfel-lows and going off at some strange tangents. And the woman hadn't even mentioned her own interest in photography. Bit odd, that, wasn't it? Odder still that she made no attempt to pass on her enthusiasm to her pupils.

DS Bridgeman looked down at his notes, then up at the assem-bled teams. He was taking the day's briefing and there was depressingly little progress to relate, but he knew better than to dwell on that lest the troops lose heart.

'There's good news from forensics about the imprints in the track through the woods,' he told them. In truth, it was mostly bad news. The ground had yielded no promising footprints, so far. 'That continuous, incised line we picked up here and there is almost definitely from a wheelbarrow.' He showed them pictures of the print. 'Joe here is following up possible makes.'

'How about footprints, Sarge?' someone asked.

'Nothing positive yet, I'm afraid.'

'Inspiration, here – I mean DC Smith,' he grinned, and corrected himself for the benefit of the outsiders, 'has been working his way through a list of missing girls and is currently following up a couple of likelies.' Or not very likelies, he thought, glumly. 'A girl from Wolverhampton and another from Heddon-on-the-Wall, in Northumbria, both have similar descriptions to the deceased.' He paused. 'There's quite a lot of progress on the pants.' That was true. The makers had been identified, but the pants were turning out to be available just about everywhere and thus it was proving hard to pinpoint where this particular pair were bought.

'As for the door-knocking, not a lot new, I'm afraid.' Oh, sod it, he put down his notes and looked hard at his weary crew. 'Now this is for your ears only.' He took a deep breath. 'As you probably all know it has come out that Rolls is not Cynthia's father but her stepfather.'

There were sidelong glances. They certainly did remember the man who, it was reputed, brought about their sergeant's most crushing defeat. Indeed, almost his *only* real defeat. 'Obviously, this makes him much more of a suspect when it comes to the disappearance of his comely stepdaughter, so I want you' – Bridgeman spoke slowly and deliberately – 'to keep Mr Rolls in mind when interviewing people. For instance, when you are taking descriptions, finding out who might have been in a certain vicinity, and so on. Many of you have seen him, but for those who haven't there is this. He held up a cutting from the *Birchfield News and Advertiser* which included a photograph taken at a St Olga's garden party on the famous brief's arrival in the area. 'I'll leave it there for you to see – but no copies.' Nobody moved or made a sound. Bridgeman glanced around. 'Is that clear?'

They all nodded.

'I'm warning you – this mustn't get out. He might be a bona-fide suspect but he's also a very dangerous customer and we don't want to alert him or bring down his wrath – right? Softly, softly is the watchword.'

Bridgeman extended his right hand to quieten other murmurs of assent and approval and sat down heavily, feeling fagged out and depressed. Well, he'd done what he could. The more he thought about it the more suspect the man Rolls became, but he could see Carol giving him an old-fashioned 'watch it' look. He appreciated that if he stuck his neck out and was proved right, he would be the hero of the hour; proved wrong, and he could be in dead trouble. Oh, what the hell. If it got the bastard who killed this girl he really didn't care about the consequences. Not just now, anyway.

Jenny stood in the once-locked room willing its spirits to tell her what to do. She was so sure in herself of what she suspected had happened, but could she convince someone else? That was the trick. She'd been in this kind of situation before when she was utterly certain of what had happened, because it had happened to her, but had failed to convince before it was too late.

What she needed to do, she decided, was to get all her evidence in order, real order, step by step, then present it to – whom? To Robin? She didn't think so. He'd look exasperated and tell her she was imagining things again. People to whom nothing threatening, violent or just plain bad had ever happened, were always like that. Always thought that other people were just making it up. They thought that evildoers must wear evil expressions or labels saying they were baddies. That they would hiss or spit or snarl, or at least have the decency to look thoroughly unpleasant. The male of the species, particularly, had no idea what it was to become a quarry, merely due to your sex or how vile even the nicest and best of cricketing chums could be when lust was upon them.

She was going off again, she knew that. Raging, Robin called it. She must not rage. She must keep calm and keep to the subject. First, Mrs Furness was not at the house when Jenny attended for interview, nor later when she arrived to house-sit. That was curious but not altogether without precedent. Both the agency owner and the relative papers had referred to Mr and Mrs Furness, although David had said Mrs Furness had left Mr Furness a little while ago. Wasn't that more curious or, as David had said, had the man not felt the need to go into personal details?

Then there was the fact that, what appeared to be Mrs Furness's clothes and jewellery, were still in the wardrobe and drawers although Jenny had to accept that these could belong to a new woman friend. But when it came to Mrs Furness's tablets – important tablets – her driving licence and passport, all still in the house. . . . But, most of all, there was the locked/unlocked room which was telling her – no – screaming at her, that something was wrong. She opened her handbag and retrieved the card DS Bridgeman had left. She dialled his number.

'There's something wrong here, I know it,' she blurted out, when she'd got through.

His mind was full of suspicions about Rolls and he responded in a deliberately calming but distant tone, 'Why do you think that, miss?'

'Well, you see' – she struggled to arrange the facts in her mind so as not to sound deranged – 'you see, it's Mrs—'

The doorbell rang. It sent her into a panic. 'Oh dear, oh dear,' she said. 'I'm sorry, doorbell has just rung.'

'Don't worry about it. I'm not going anywhere,' Bridgeman assured her. 'Just ring me back as soon as you are free again.' Then he rang off.

It was only as she was hurrying down the stairs that Jenny thought to be nervous about who might be on the other side of the front door. Casual callers did not usually find their way down this lonely lane.

'Who is it?' she shouted, failing to hide all the tremble in her voice.

The woman's voice which responded was firm and confident. 'I might well make that enquiry of you.' Then she added. 'This is Georgina, Georgina Furness.' There was a pause. 'Well,' she enquired crisply, 'well, aren't you going to let me into my house?'

10

They were in serious need of a breakthrough, thought Bridgeman as he sifted through the scant information coming in. He was on auto pilot as he made decisions on some things and put others aside until he could parley with DI Glass.

Rolls was still very much on his mind. There was something he should be grasping there, he was sure, but it kept floating away out of reach. What was it? Rolls was the stepfather right, not, as he had led them to presume, the father, right. Odd of him not to say? Yes. The man must know of the suspicions that fell even more readily on stepfathers than fathers? Good reason not to say, maybe. Might cloud the issue? Rolls, the sophisticated man who had dragged himself to this backwater to be near his beautiful stepdaughter. If he was going to get a place in the country, surely horsy Hampshire or wealthy Sussex would be more the thing? They could always move the girl to another school?

Rolls, was the only one at home when Cynthia went missing. What if she had returned home that day? They only had Rolls's word that she hadn't. Hadn't Rolls exercised all his considerable talents on saving that toad Hayden, making full use of Hayden's completely fictitious defence – possibly even assisting in its fabrication? Rolls would claim he was merely doing his job, whilst Bridgeman would be the first to admit that everyone deserves a fair trial and a reasonable defence, even vicious, multiple rapists.

But what if there were more to it than that? What if Rolls were that way inclined himself? Got off on defending such people, or even gathered a few tips? Maybe made some good connections. Perversions made strange bedfellows and he had the feeling that, in this case, if it *were* all one case, more than one pair of hands and one brain were involved. That's why it was so impenetrable. Too many strands here and too few clues left for one person to have managed it alone, but at least with such a wide canvas, they couldn't keep their eyes on all the cracks forming. If they were not in constant touch, doubt and confusion could set in. Well, the cracks had better start appearing soon. But maybe Rolls was like Hayden, a loner. It was part of his MO, and part of his protection. No stranger rapist he. No leaping at a woman out of a dark alley for him. He had wanted, indeed he seemed to require, that the victim fall for him, or at least be very taken, bedazzled by his good looks and caring charm. True, at the start, the women always had been strangers to him. What's more, they were always attractive women, which seemed to make their degradation more appealing to him.

His charm and looks had been such a wonderful defence. What need had he to rape? Then, went his story, when he no longer wished to carry on the affair – which he had only undertaken out of pity, really – she seeks revenge – and look what a neurotic woman she is? Hell hath no fury, etc.

This scenario was brilliantly put across and embellished by a clever barrister like Rolls, who seemed to care not one whit what the man had done. He had managed to get the four cases, with which Bridgeman had charged Hayden, heard separately so the jury in each case had no idea that this delightful man made a habit of such things. Rolls was an attractive man, too. . . .

What he needed to do was find out more about Rolls's similar cases. Did any of the defendants live around here? They'd looked at the convicted, but what about the other bastards he'd got off? One thing was certain: if Bridgeman was to pursue this line of enquiry strongly at this early stage, he was going to have to cross every t and dot every i. If pursuing Hayden on a hunch was dodgy, doing the same with Rolls would be suicidal. Not only would people think it was sour grapes, due to his defeat at the man's hands, but Rolls would make a formidable foe.

He was still trying to decide whether he was being paranoid about this man when he suddenly realized that that woman at Berry Hill House had not yet rung him back. She'd said there was something wrong, sounded panicky, then there had been a ring on the doorbell.

Christ! She was stuck out there in the middle of nowhere. She'd given a shout for help...! He rang her number. It was engaged. He left it for three minutes, meanwhile drumming his fingers on the desk and snatching impatient glances at his watch. He rang again. Still engaged. The telephone company took their time informing him there was, in fact, nobody on the line. By then he was running down the stairs, mobile phone clamped to his ear. He'd been sitting there cogitating about Rolls and ignoring a cry for help!

Carol, who was, as usual, breathlessly ascending the stairs for her health's sake, was startled to see this apparition fly past, beckoning her to follow him.

'Something's come up,' he yelled, unnecessarily.

En route he filled her in.

'Phone knocked off the rest, I expect,' Carol said unsympathetically. 'Jackie and Bella do it all the time. Jackie thinks it's an extension of her arm.'

'Hmm. Maybe.'

He was belting through Hartmeet at rather more than thirty miles an hour. Would she survive the ten miles from Birchfield to Berry Hill House, Carol wondered? As a distraction, Carol brought him up to date with her photo news; that there was, in fact, a chap who had often used double spots, but he didn't attend the club any more. She had his address. Then, the surprising news that the snooty headmistress was a member. A keen photographer who did not feel her hobby was sufficiently interesting to become a part of their leisure curriculum.

Bridgeman shook his head as he did an almost screeching left turn to go north on the Louden road. 'This case gets weirder and weirder.' He banged on the steering wheel. 'Come on! Come on!' Then almost to himself, 'God, I hope we are in time; I'll never forgive myself if anything's happened to Jenny.'

Carol was startled by the mention of the woman's first name. As far as she knew, Bridgeman and the lady house-sitter had met only once. Besides which, names were not the DS's strong suit – a cause of much ribbing from the troops. 'That's all you need,' they would mutter, – 'a detective sergeant with a rotten memory for names.'

Jenny had been in a daze from the moment she had opened the door to find a good-looking, fortyish, cashmere-sweatered and calf-booted lady on the step. She felt decidedly at a disadvantage being faced with the woman who, a few minutes earlier, she was sure must be dead, murdered even.

As it was, Jenny could not imagine that the woman sitting opposite her might need anyone's protection much less that of a scaredy-cat like her. Direct and forthright would be an accurate description of Mrs Furness or, as Robin would put it, she was 'a no-messing lady'. Not exactly an overbearing, well-to-do, county lady, unaccustomed to resistance from the lower orders, more the kindly but firm nursing sister who demanded your pink card and wanted to know whether you had seen doctor.

With this for-your-own-good manner she had extracted all Jenny's credentials and her situation within the first few minutes of their chat. No matter how intrusive the questions of such direct people, Jenny had noticed, one felt obliged to answer them. Maybe their obvious need to have all the facts at their fingertips banished any suspicion of mere nosiness or ulterior motive.

From her passport Jenny was pretty certain that it was Mrs Furness that she saw before her but, nonetheless, felt she should do her house-sitter's duty. While she poured a second cup of lapsang souchong she cleared her throat before saying in a firm voice, 'Would you show me some proof of your identity, please?'

The pink-and-white flowered tea-cup froze *en route* to Georgina Furness's discreetly painted mouth.

'You appreciate,' went on Jenny, braver now with the bit between her teeth, 'that this house has been left in my care by Mr Furness, and since I have never met you before. . . .'

To Jenny's relief the woman smiled, a surprisingly warm and winning smile. She was handsome rather than pretty, Jenny decided, with her silver-streaked, no-nonsense bob and healthy glow.

'Of course, my dear.' She put down her cup. 'How very sensible of you and how very silly of me not to think of that.' She picked up her black calf bag which, if Jenny were any judge, must be worth four times her weekly grocery bill. 'I can't show you a driving licence, I'm afraid. I mislaid that some time ago. But I do have my cheque book and cards.' She released a waterfall of credit cards from a neat black calf folder inscribed with a gold monogram, GF.

'I have to admit, when I stormed out I didn't exactly think to go through all the drawers to check if I had all my documents.' She smiled a conspiratorial woman-to-woman smile. 'I didn't want to ruin my dramatic exit.' They both laughed. Jenny felt herself warming to this strong lady. She had a twinkle in her eye and, Jenny felt sure, no malice in her soul.

'Your driving licence is in the jewellery drawer in the master bedroom,' she confided, then blushed. 'I only saw it,' she added hurriedly, 'because I opened the drawer to tuck in a scarf which was hanging out – and then I saw all your interesting hand-crafted jewellery. . . .'

'Jewellery? Not mine, my dear,' Georgina Furness interrupted. 'I took all my loot with me; I did make sure of that. Must belong to his latest floozie. One of a long line.' She leaned over and patted Jenny's hand. 'And don't worry that I might think you go around poking into other people's business: I'm certain I would!'

Bridgeman was out of the car almost before he had brought it to a standstill. There were no strange vehicles on the gravel standing and the exterior of Berry Hill House presented a closed and silent front.

Banging on the front door and ringing the doorbell brought no response. He dashed around to join Carol at the back. As before, the kitchen door was open. Inside, no one. They both ran from room to room shouting Jenny's name. Upstairs, in a spare room, they found a phone knocked off its rest. Back in the kitchen they paused for breath.

'Looks bad?' asked Carol. She spotted the tea tray loaded with pink-and-white teapot; two used, pink-flowered cups, saucers and tea plates and a larger plate containing three homemade biscuits. 'She's certainly had visitors,' Carol commented, feeling the teapot, 'but this is cold now.' Then she spotted a wide roll of brown sticky tape and a pair of scissors and said, 'Uh huh. Look at this.'

Though ominous to Carol, the sight of these objects seemed to make Bridgeman relax a little. 'Don't worry. I know where she is,' he said. 'At least, I think I do.' He dashed off down the garden path and into the greenhouse, causing a startled Jenny to smudge a deep pink cyclamen petal which she had been hoping to paint in one transparent application.

'Damn!' she exclaimed then looked up. When she saw who it . was she exclaimed furiously, 'You've bloody well done it again! I don't believe it! For someone who claims to know about painting, Sergeant Bridgeman, you have a funny way of showing it!'

Then she registered his concerned, overwrought face and noticed how breathless they both were.

'Oh dear,' she said, putting her brush down. Pink spots were creeping on to her cheeks. 'Oh dear,' she said again. 'My fault?'

Jenny's delectable home-made biscuits were beginning to bring about a thaw.

'I'm really sorry I didn't phone you back,' she said contritely for the third time. 'But as you can imagine I was just amazed to find Mrs Furness at the door – and I had no idea I'd knocked the phone off the rest.'

Bridgeman waved away the latest apology. 'One of those things.' He paused. 'What you haven't told us is, what was wrong? You said, "something has happened".'

A pink flush began creeping its way up her neck. She'd obviously been dreading this.

'It seems so silly now. I can hardly bring myself to tell you.'

'We all do silly things at times,' murmured Carol in her most motherly fashion.

'I thought something had happened to Mrs Furness,' Jenny confessed. She explained the sequence of events.

They didn't laugh, or seem annoyed, or tell Jenny she was a silly hysterical woman, as Robin had that morning.

'Hunches can prove right,' shrugged Bridgeman. 'We have to play them all the time. Hard work and hunches that's what it's all about. Mustn't worry about feeling a fool.' He didn't add that he had felt and still did feel that there was something odd about this house and atmosphere. But maybe he was just tuning into her vibes.

'I'm only sorry Mrs Furness has gone,' he said. 'I'd have liked to have asked her about Linda.'

'Oh, I told her that,' said Jenny, clearly relieved to have got something right. 'I gave her your name and telephone number and she said she would get in touch.'

'Did she say when?'

'Well, I did tell her it was urgent. Of course, she had heard about Linda being missing but said it was unlikely she could tell you anything because the girl had stopped coming a couple of months before she left. Too busy with exams or something.'

'Mrs Furness leave an address?'

'No, I'm afraid not. I did ask her, but she said she was on the move too much at the moment.'

Hmm, thought Bridgeman. Slippery customers, these Furnesses.

11

'I think I've got something, Sarge,' announced Doggie Edwards, in his most earnest manner. Then he thought better of it and added cautiously, 'Well, maybe.'

'Don't worry,' Bridgeman assured him, 'I'm easily pleased right now. Give.'

'The girl's pants,' said Doggie. He shrank from calling them knickers in case it seemed too flippant. 'You know they said they were sold all over the place?'

'I certainly do,' said Bridgeman, gesturing for the over-serious young man to stop hovering and sit. 'Very depressing news, that was.'

'Well, just on the off-chance we asked the makers to do us a south-east only run-down. And the result was that they found that not many shops in the area ordered the pants in ecru.'

'What's that, for Christ's sake?'

'Sort of beige – which was the colour the girl was wearing.'

'Oh, right.'

'Apparently, it proved a bit of a non-runner sales-wise. All due, as the sales director put it, to a breakdown in intelligence.'

'What does that mean, in plain English?'

'That the women who wear this sort of skimpy thong-thing didn't like it in that colour. They thought it looked a bit grubby. The makers were choked because they'd sold lots of a similar colour called natural but that was a bit more pinky.'

'I'm with you so far.'

'Well, for some weird reason they did sell one large batch of this ecru – to a shop called Knickers-U-Like, in Headington.'

That made Bridgeman sit up. Headington was only twenty-seven miles north-east of Birchfield. The nearest, decent-sized, shopping town, it boasted branches of all the main clothing outlets. 'Heading for Headington' was the locals' way of saying we're off for a good shop.

'The batch they ordered was in sizes eight and ten and, as you know, the victim was wearing size ten.'

'I like the sound of this,' said Bridgeman encouragingly. 'What do Knickers-U-Like have to say about who bought them?'

'I'm just off to see them now.'

'Good.'

Bridgeman felt better. It wasn't much but it was something. If it narrowed the field down to local girls, that alone would be a big plus. Up to now, they had imagined that she couldn't be local. Otherwise, surely someone would have come forward, not necessarily to claim her but at least to say they recognized the description? Thus they were thinking, depressingly, of a coun-trywide catchment area. That she might even have been dropped here by some long-distance lorry driver or travelling salesman. What a bummer that could be, the victim neither local nor killed in the vicinity.

But, if she *was* local, why was there no missing person index tie-up? Because she was past the age of consent and didn't want anyone to know where she was? Or her nearest and dearest didn't even know she was missing? Which could mean she did live locally but originally came from somewhere else. A hotel worker? A student at the Poly? Surely there had been enough publicity to make those non-runners? It was a great puzzle.

Carol came breezing in looking optimistic.

'You got me some good news too?' asked Bridgeman hope-fully.

'Dunno. But it just occurred to me – when I saw the ghastly stuff Jackie was putting on her fingers – is anyone on to the victim's nail varnish?'

The girl's nails had been painted a dark olive green shot with iridescent flecks. At least they had been when lit up by an ultra-violet inspection lamp. Later, in the daylight, a magical change occurred when it became light green with gold flecks. Spooky.

Bridgeman shook his head. 'No,' he admitted. 'Not yet. I've got it in mind but there are so many cosmetic outlets I've put it on the back burner for now.' He paused. 'You on to something then?'

'Well, I described it to Jackie and she had never seen or heard of such a polish – and she's a world expert believe me. Way-out nail varnish is her latest craze – God knows where I've gone wrong. At least Bella wouldn't be seen dead wearing the stuff. Anyway, she does know about one which changes from pink to purple but not one from dark to light green and back again.'

Bridgeman was puzzled. 'Why would they want it to change and when would they be under ultra-violet light for it to be seen?'

Carol shook her head at his ignorance. 'For a bit of a lark when they go clubbing of course, and that's where—'

'They have ultra-violet lights,' he finished for her.

'Anyway,' Carol continued, 'I popped into Angel Faces, that posh pharmacy in Chapel Street and the cosmetic counters in local stores, but none of the assistants had seen anything like the varnish I described. So, it's obviously some special brand – maybe theatrical – or is just produced by a small company.'

'I knew there had to be some good reason for allowing a devoted mum on the team,' teased Bridgeman. He was beginning to feel even better. 'So, the nail varnish trail it is.' He looked at her hopefully. 'Needs a woman's touch as you've already demonstrated.'

'Sorry, Sarge, I'm too tied up on my photo kick. But I will ask the parents about the nail varnish.'

'Add ecru knickers while you're at it,' muttered Bridgeman and ambled over to the TIE man to get his nail-varnish data doled out elsewhere. He was followed by Carol murmuring, 'Ecru knickers? What are you on about? Is this the male menopause kicking in or what?'

'Ecru,' said Bridgeman with a certain smugness, 'is another name for beige.'

'I know what ecru is!' exclaimed Carol. 'But it's an old fashioned name for the colour of a modern pair of knickers. It's usually something more like champagne, pearl or flesh.'

'I'll store that vital information away in my dirty old man's treasure chest. Meanwhile, if you refuse to help your old sarge with this urgent nail varnish ID you might give some womanly thought as to why these ecru knickers might sell well in Headington but nowhere else.' He paused. 'Odd that, don't you think?'

'Bloody weird if you ask me.'

Jenny draped a white and purple shawl over an occasional table, ensuring that the fine wool material fell into appropriately artistic folds. Then she hung a pale acid-yellow throw over the blackboard in the background, draping it to one side. Out of her holdall she took a small, pale-green jug, a brass candlestick and a tall, fat-bellied, earthenware pot and positioned them on the shawl. She made sure their outlines overlapped from whichever angle they were viewed. This was not intended to be a difficult exercise in composition but an experiment in colour handling.

When the first of her ten pupils arrived she was busy inserting bulrushes, and purple and pale-yellow iris flags into the tall pot and brazenly multi-coloured primulas into the jug when the first of her ten pupils arrived. Not all of the class attended every time but most did, being painfully aware that if the numbers fell too low the class might be axed.

'A colour challenge, today, I see,' murmured Mrs Petty, as she unloaded her neat painting pack and began arranging the contents on one of the desks near Jenny's still-life.

'I don't think the likes of you needs it, frankly,' said Jenny apologetically.

Mrs Petty was a small woman with a slight mid-European accent and a quite considerable talent for turning out tiny pictures in jewel-like colours.

93

'Ah, but it stretches me to tackle someone else's arrangement,' she said generously. 'Otherwise I'd go on painting the colour combinations I know go well.'

The others began filtering in. First, Mr Archibald, a finicky, retired surveyor who was really rather sweet and, oddly, painted wildly bizarre pictures. Then Helen Fairweather and Georgina Banks, two lively but horribly bored young housewives escaping howling babies for one night each week. Helen, who came just for the company, dabbled happily and with good humour and chatted to the others whenever she could. Georgina, on the other hand, had proved to be a natural. She had talent and just seemed to drop into the loose, imaginative style others strove for ceaselessly, and to use colour combinations so daring that even Jenny would never dream of trying them.

Next, into Perival School's shabby and rather chilly room, came Ellie Prinks, a knowing young woman who had attended art school. This, she clearly felt, placed her more than a cut above the rest. Jenny was convinced that Ellie only turned up to get her regular superiority fix. She stalked around the room, head to one side then the other, knees bent then straightened perusing the set-up from every view, so as to establish the best possible angle before choosing her seat, then deliberately moving it, noisily, to a more suitable spot. All of this was to illustrate that she was a proper artist.

However, the preening Ellie was little problem compared with the next arrival whom Jenny would have been happy not to see at all, even at the cost of cutting her precious numbers. She was the gaunt, elderly, ever-complaining Mrs Hedges. Mrs Hedges was possessed of not an iota of natural talent, but was nonetheless totally resistant to the idea that she might work hard and practise to compensate for this lack. She merely waited for Jenny to impart her secret of how she painted so professionally without any effort whatsoever, a secret she was certain Jenny was deliberately withholding out of spite and jealousy.

Finally, came her most favourite attendee: Eddie Bates, a burly truck driver who liked most of all to paint delicate flowers. He often brought her little posies culled from wayside halts. Jenny would have loved to see the reaction of his fellow drivers to this endearing little habit.

Seven; not bad. That would probably be the lot for that evening. If they were coming at all they were usually here by now. Jenny began her introductory lead-in.

'As you can see I've set you a bit of a colour challenge. Up to now you've been using a limited palette which is very good practice but when it comes to flowers you'll find it's not always so easy to mix all the colours you want, particularly clear purples, mauves and lilacs . . .'

As she spoke the door opened tentatively. She'd been wrong. A latecomer.

'. . . that's why I asked you to add a couple of new colours. . . .'

A man's head peeped around the door. It was surrounded by black curls and its face wore a beguiling smile.

'Sorry to disturb you, teacher,' murmured David, 'but I'd like to join your class.'

Bridgeman was not a natural sidler-up to topics. His preference was straight from the shoulder. But eight years in the CID had tempered that natural inclination. A detective who couldn't sidle up to a topic, approach it obliquely as though by chance, didn't stand an earthly. He might as well dust down his uniform and say farewell.

Thus it was two hours on, in an evening which had begun its alcoholic progress at 7.30 p.m., before he sidled up to his main reason for getting together with his old pal, Harry Meadows. Harry was a solicitor. But Harry had sat next to Bridgeman from Class 4a on at Headington Comprehensive and watched him making pellets with which to torment Swotty Beckworth, so knew him too well to be fooled by this prevarication.

He swallowed a mouthful of the Red Lion's delicious steak and kidney pie, took a swig of its best bitter and muttered,

'Look, Derek, if you want the low-down on Rolls why don't you just ask me?'

'You know why.'

'Well.' Harry glanced around. 'There is just you and me here. We're old pals and' – he pushed back his heavily framed specs – worn partly to give his baby face some gravitas – 'you're not asking me to break any of the legal profession's boy scout rules, are you, for heaven's sake?'

He grinned as he picked up his glass then added, 'Mind you, I'm not sure I know that much about the man.'

'Any morsel gratefully accepted. Particularly of a personal nature.'

'Well, I know he's been married before. But I suppose you've already guessed that. I don't know the woman's name or where-abouts, but I could make some discreet enquiries.'

'Be grateful,' said Bridgeman. 'Any gossip about him? Any of those unfounded sexual harassment complaints from female pupils or office staff?'

'You're getting to be such a cynic, Sergeant Bridgeman.'

'You would say that, wouldn't you?' Bridgeman murmured. 'How about background. Filthy rich?'

'Oh no. Come up from nuffink, I understand. Well, maybe not exactly nothing, but from struggling, lower-middle class. Father was a civil servant, mother a nurse. He was an only child.'

Bridgeman put his hand up to stop his friend in full flow. 'You knew I was going to pump you about him, didn't you?'

Harry grinned and patted his arm. 'Had an idea. I'm not a detective but, you know. . . .' He shrugged. 'Not so hard to figure. So, I did a bit of homework, just in case.'

Bridgeman shook his head and grinned at his old school chum. 'Appreciate it.'

Harry waved away his thanks.

'Well then, care to go into the black box?'

'Fire away.'

'Career?' asked Bridgeman.

'Onward and upward without a backward glance, I gather.'

'Does he specialize? Fraud, murder, rape?'

'Dunno. I only know the stuff he's doing on this circuit, but I'll make a few enquiries.'

'Discreet.'

'What else? I'm entitled – might want to use him for a client.'

'Have you ever?'

'No.'

'Why not?'

'Dunno really. No particular reason, I suppose. We're just a bit locked into a couple of other good mouthpieces.'

'One other thing, then I'll let you get on with your steak and kidney.'

'Fire away.'

Bridgeman paused and took a deep breath for the big one. 'Know why he came to live here?'

'Daughter's school nearby, wasn't it?'

'That's the story.'

'Could be true. Not everything a brief says is a lie, you know, old pal,' said Meadows. 'And, yes, I will have another.' He pushed his glass forward before resolutely tucking back into his pie.

'No wonder they called you the champion chomper at school,' muttered Bridgeman.

It had been such a lovely warm day and she'd been so enjoying doing such a simple everyday thing like taking a cool shower after gardening. Suddenly, Aden Bullen was in the bathroom, pulling the curtain aside and reaching greedily for her breasts and snarling, 'You've been dying for it, now you're going to get it!'

She was transfixed with surprise. Was it a joke? How could it be, what he was doing now – pulling at her. . . . She resisted. Oh how she resisted once she recovered from her shock, but he had her at such a disadvantage and he was so strong! He'd dragged her out of the shower taking no heed as she crashed against the metal surrounds, then slammed her up against the tiled bathroom wall.

'Stop that screaming!' he yelled, shaking her. 'There's no one here!' She knew he was right and had begun to sob as she fought.

It could not have been a better scenario for a rapist she realized later. She unclothed, stunned, confused and so much weaker than him. He had no trousers on she realized when she'd become aware of his obscene erection already in place. She tried to knee him in the crotch but slipped on the wet floor. That was when he hit her, quite hard, knocking her to the floor and dazing her.

Then his heavy weight was pinning her down, his foul beery breath in her face and his rough hands thrusting her legs apart as he called her a whore, a filthy whore. And it was done.

Robin had had a bad day in town chasing elusive jobs. Now, thought Jenny, he's taking it out on me. Well, she wasn't having it this time. At least he'd been out socializing while she had been slogging away at her despised daubs and teaching to earn the money for the long lunches – which seemed so vital for landing a job in advertising.

What's more, he didn't appear to worry about her being alone at Berry Hill House which, given her experience, was thoughtless to say the least. In fact, he didn't seem in the least interested in what she had been doing. It was his way, he said when tackled, to stop her dwelling on things. So she was obliged to listen endlessly to the latest news on his old pal, Vince Power's love life and Henry's latest, mind-blowing campaign for breakfast cheese whirly toasts. How, at the very last minute, just as they were about to start a presentation and with a head of mud after a heavy night, the brilliant slogan, Try A Whirly Early! had just popped into Vince's mind. The delighted clients had been convinced he'd been slogging away for months on the idea. Robin, she sometimes felt, was like a bedazzled juvenile when it came to tales about whizz kids Vince and Henry.

'Can you believe what Henry did then?' was one of Robin's cries, when describing the man's latest sortie or jape or the pulling of a campaign out of the fire. She found it embarrassing to watch him getting worked up about that silly, self-regarding man. If he was so clever why couldn't he find a job for Robin? But up to now she felt it her duty to look duly impressed. Perhaps she should never have started, but it was a habit hard to break. As she watched Robin, spluttering through the latest Vince and Henry sagas, she noticed he wasn't meeting her eye. Was there more to these jaunts than she had realized? Was he up to his old tricks again?

Since the last time, he had sworn he would be faithful for ever. Burbled on about how hard it was for an even remotely attractive man to resist the temptations in advertising, where even the office juniors were stunning. 'We don't employ ugly birds', was one of the less charming chants of the wonderful Vince, himself a quite unsavoury-looking person. Then there was the bonding with colleagues which, Robin pointed out, inevitably occurred when you are working your butt off together and throwing your heart and soul into an important campaign pitch. 'You get this . . . buzz. . . .'

He wasn't actually working in advertising any more, but lots of the temptations must remain, and now he had plenty of time to indulge them. He was certainly an attractive man, she sighed to herself, with what he so unattractively termed 'knicker-pulling power'. Tall, slim and dark. A little on the too sleek and slick side, she'd thought, when she'd first met him. But that had been before she had been subjected to the full flattery of his barrage of sincere attention. She now realized that that had probably kicked in because of her obvious resistance to his charms.

Part of his 'campaign strategy' had been an ardent interest in her artistic talent which he now judged entirely by its commercial worth. By his lights that, and only that, gave it suitable meaning and gravity. If it didn't sell for megabucks it was not worth anything. How different to David. Once he'd got around to enrolling, he had drunk in her advice and watched her demonstrations with awe. Of course, that, too, might be a stance. Maybe he, too, would dismiss her talents at a later stage in the relationship. Here, wait a minute, she said to herself. What relationship? He wanted to learn from her, that was all. Clearly, he already had something of a flair and she was happy to teach such an eager and cheerful pupil. That was all and the fact that he made her class number up to eleven was an added bonus.

Despite the shop's title, when Doggie had blithely said he was off to talk to the owner of Knickers-U-Like he had not envisaged himself, a young man of serious and even studious mien, in such an overwhelmingly alien ambiance. There he stood, in his grey bomber jacket, grey trousers, cream shirt and discreet tie, totally surrounded by knickers. Satin knickers, lacy knickers, frilly knickers, sleek knickers, big knickers and knickers so small that, they scarcely existed – all crammed in rack upon rack into a tiny premises on Chantry Street. Towering above him were huge blow-ups of almost nude young women wearing knickers which only evidenced themselves by glimpses of either tiny triangles of material at the front or a fraction of thong emerging from provocative buttocks at the back.

The girl behind the counter gave him an unfriendly stare. Doggie was often given the undercover jobs and enquiries where a mildly anoraked/nerd image would not stand out. Not so this time. The saleswoman, he was painfully aware, clearly thought he was one of those men who came in to the shop just to get a rush out of riffling feverishly through piles of skimpy knickers.

'Yes?' she said coldly.

'Mrs Venderamee, please.' He pulled out his warrant card and showed it to the girl, although there was no need as he had an appointment. 'She's expecting me.'

He had vaguely expected Mrs Venderamee to be wearing a sari, but she turned out to be a smartly and firmly suited Jewish businesswoman, with a very direct expression. The aura she gave off was co-operative but watchful – clearly aware that their discussion could result in bad publicity, but also that being obstructive was not an option.

She offered Doggie a coffee. He declined, then explained his quest in more detail than he had on the phone. She had already looked up the order number and she knew her stock.

'I remember the line well,' she said. 'Even though it was nine months ago.' She smiled slightly. 'A very misguided design/colour combination I must tell you.'

'In what way?'

'They looked almost invisible when a girl put them on.'

Doggie was nonplussed. He glanced up at the near-naked bottoms on the posters which could be glimpsed through the ribbon curtains of her cupboard-like office, spread his hands and said, 'But. . . .'

'Oh yes, Officer, I know they almost look as if they have none on, but the operative word is "almost". What there is of them they *want* to be seen. Partly, just to show that they *are* wearing knickers, and partly as a sort of trimming around the desirable parts on show. Other colours in this style sold well.'

Doggie felt out of his depth. Really, a woman officer should have been doing this enquiry but he had wanted to follow it through himself – doggie-like.

'So why did you order them? If you thought they were—'

'An abomination?' She paused. 'Well, since we're a knickers only shop I feel we ought to give all colours in any new line a try. We can be wrong and miss a trend. For example, I never thought big knickers would come back. So, anyway, I ordered a half-dozen each of size eight and ten in these ecru thongs and, as I expected, they stuck. No interest whatsoever. I was about to send them back – we have a special sale or return arrangement with the suppliers since we're such a good outlet for them and they can use us as a testing ground. Then, suddenly, someone came in and bought the lot. I have to tell you, I was amazed.'

Doggie was now leaning forward, trying not to let his excitement show.

'This customer,' he said softly, 'was it a man or a woman?'

Mrs Venderamee pursed her lips and shook her head. 'We do promise privacy and discretion to our customers, particularly

101

male customers.'

Well, that was one question answered. The buyer was a man. 'What was he like?'

She hesitated. 'It was a long time ago.'

'Mrs Venderamee,' said Doggie, suddenly the firm policeman, 'you *must* tell us what you know. This is a very serious matter.' He could be quite intimidating when the bone was in sight. 'If you withhold evidence now it could reflect quite badly on your business when the truth comes out – as it inevitably will. On the other hand, any co-operation would be warmly acknowledged should you so wish.'

She listened carefully weighing up what he was saying. He'd sensed where her priorities lay, with her business. Now he played the conscience card.

'Besides which, would you ever forgive yourself if another girl was murdered and you hadn't told what you know?'

He was not to know that Mrs Venderamee had a teenage daughter.

'To be absolutely honest with you,' she said, 'I don't remember much about him except that he was tall, well-dressed, dark-haired and seemed quite ... educated. He spoke nicely,' she explained.

'Thin? Fat? Middling?'

'Oh lean, definitely on the lean side, although he was bundled up because it was winter.'

'Cash, card or cheque?' Doggie kept his fingers crossed but it availed him nothing.

'Cash. I've checked back.'

He hid his disappointment. 'Would you recognize him again?'

She grimaced and sighed. 'I really don't know.' She contemplated his eager, intense face then suddenly gave him a motherly smile. 'But I would certainly do my best, Officer.'

12

'I think she's my sister,' said the young woman, pushing the artist's impression back across the interview-room table. She had Glass and Bridgeman's undivided attention.

'Your sister's gone missing?' asked Glass.

She nodded glumly. 'And that looks almost like her' – she pointed to the picture – 'and the description fits – apart from the hair colouring.'

Their informant was tall and probably no more than about twenty-five, but had a strained expression and a tired look about the eyes which made her appear older. She wore trim navy-blue trousers and a scarlet jacket with a gold shield on the breast pocket. Circled around the shield was the word SELECT.

Glass raised a hand. 'Sorry, before you go on, can you tell me why you have taken so long to come forward?'

'I work abroad. I'm a travel courier.' She pointed to her badge. 'I've been in the Far East for the last six months.'

'You don't read English newspapers while you're away?'

She sighed and shook her head. 'The only things I read are the lists of incoming passengers, their special needs and their itineraries. It's a very busy job and I'm constantly on the move.'

Glass gestured for her to continue. Their surname was Scanscomber she revealed. Her first name was Hazel and that of her seventeen-year-old sister, Avril. Both their parents were dead. They had been killed in a car crash some eighteen months earlier. At that time, they had been living on the Rainby estate

103

just outside Birchfield. Hazel was already working in the travel business and had just been offered the opportunity to handle up-market, long-haul trips. Quite a leg up for a girl from the Rainby.

'Taking up the offer meant leaving Avril on her own but she insisted I took my opportunity,' explained Hazel sadly. 'She could have gone to live with our Auntie Rita and Uncle George, but we've never been close and he always came on to us a bit. Avril had worked as a nursery nurse, so she became a live-in nanny for friends in Liverpool instead.' She shrugged. 'It seemed a good idea at the time. But things did not go as smoothly as we'd hoped,' Hazel admitted.

Her careful speech must have been acquired on the road to self-improvement, thought Bridgeman. 'People have pointed out since that going to work for friends can be a mistake,' she went on. 'But we didn't realize that at the time. Avril rang me after she and Janey – that's the wife – had had a serious disagreement. But I was out – meeting the latest arrivals.' Her nails dug into her palms as she recalled the incident that would probably go over and over in her mind for the rest of her life. 'So, she left a message saying she was leaving. She had another possibility in mind, she said. Something marvellous – if it worked out. I was not to worry, she would get in touch again when she was settled. She sounded quite excited.'

'That was – when?' asked Glass.

'Three months ago.'

Hazel's face like the rest of her was big but only kept from prettiness by her quite large, straight nose. She was well groomed and had a certain presence. At first, there seemed to be little resemblance between her and her more delicately put-together, younger sister. But when she turned her head sideways, Bridgeman could see a similarity around the mouth – that slightly protruding, pouting effect. The resemblance became more obvious when Hazel showed them photographs of her and Avril, looking younger, cavorting and giggling in their back garden. In them, for the first time, Bridgeman saw the victim animated. It was always difficult to make a corpse come alive.

Try as he might, Bridgeman had found that he just couldn't 'see' Avril's blank, lifeless face laughing, crying, eating – just being. Now he could, and it was heartbreaking.

'Have you any professional portraits of Avril?' he blurted out, only to be rewarded with an icy glance from Glass.

Hazel was puzzled, 'No . . . ?'

Glass intervened. 'Before we go any further' – he reached for Hazel's hand and held it in his own immaculately manicured fingers – 'are you up to identifying the body now?'

'You mean, right now?' The voice was cracking. Showing sympathy at this moment seemed not to be a good idea but maybe Glass had a purpose. In any case, the girl's courier training seemed to be standing her in good stead. She sat up a little straighter and held her head high.

'Yes.' She paused. 'In fact I was hoping to do that as soon as possible.' Her words were coming out slowly now, automaton-like. 'I want to know, one way or another.' She stopped, then it spilled out in a rush, 'She's all I've got, you know.' Her voice finally broke and the tears flowed.

Some people get more than their fair share of woe, Bridgeman reflected. First, both parents wiped out in one fell swoop and, so soon after, the only remaining, close relative done to death deliberately and violently. Not surprisingly, Hazel was in a kind of daze and shivering slightly as they stood over the body.

'Was she. . . ?'

'Raped?'

She nodded, wordlessly.

Bridgeman shook his head. 'No, we don't think so.' He didn't mention that she appeared to have had recent sex, or that they had found semen in both her vagina and her mouth – from two different sources. Also, a mighty dose of drugs in her system. No sense in piling on the agony unnecessarily.

'We're going to need you,' Bridgeman now told Hazel.

'Anything,' she replied, gazing down at her dead sister for the last time, 'anything.'

105

'When can we have a long talk?'

'Now.' She was in a daze but a certain steeliness had crept into her voice and manner. Bridgeman recognized the auto-pilot mode adopted by relatives who were prepared to drive themselves on, despite awful pain, to ensure justice was done for a nearest and dearest. 'Tears can come later,' Hazel murmured, reading his mind. He was glad she had a hectic job to return to. Being busy helped a great deal at bad times.

Despite the self-imposed rigour, Hazel stumbled as they left the mortuary and had to be supported back to the car. 'A little later will do,' he assured her.

'No, now.'

It appeared that Avril had been just an ordinary teenage girl with ordinary interests: clothes, make-up, pop idols and boys. Hazel was not aware of any particular boyfriend.

'How about hobbies?' asked Carol, who had been called in to play the eternal mum.

'None, really,' Hazel said. She thought a bit then offered, 'She liked drawing. She did quite well in art class.' She hesitated again, as though trying to drag the vision of her sister back into her mind, then said, 'But, of course, how stupid of me. There were the animals.'

'She had pets?'

'Oh no, we couldn't. We did have a cat, Pearly, but Avril couldn't take her to Liverpool because of the baby – so we had to bequeath her to a neighbour.'

'Could she have gone back to see it, as well as her chum?'

'Yes. I know she did see Pearly a couple of times because she wrote and told me. But what she did mostly with animals was to give a hand at the Springfield Park Animal Rescue Centre.'

'Oh, that's interesting,' said Carol, leaning forward encouragingly. 'What did she do there?'

'All sorts of odd jobs. Cleaning out the stables and kennels, feeding animals – but mostly taking dogs for walks.'

Well, this might be an interesting slant, but Bridgeman failed to see how it tied up with Linda and Cynthia, except that Cynthia liked riding.

'Wonder she didn't get a job there,' said Carol.

'Oh, she wanted to,' exclaimed Hazel, 'she would have loved that, but' – she sat back heavily – 'there were no full-time vacancies. They did say she would be top of the list when any came up, though.' For a moment she sounded proud and hopeful, then reality seeped back.

Quickly, Carol switched the subject. 'And friends, did she have many?'

'Yes. Well, quite a few.'

Bridgeman pushed over his notepad, 'Would you list as many as you can remember, please. Oh, and put crosses next to the more important ones.'

Hazel reached for her black leather tote bag and took out a sleek, silver pen. Obviously part of her armoury as a top travel courier. She began writing then stopped. 'This won't be right up to date. I had already gone before she left for Liverpool.'

Bridgeman waved away her doubts. 'Don't worry. It'll be a start. Up to now, we've had nothing.'

'Oh, and another thing,' said Hazel, 'she did know that missing girl, Linda.'

Jenny just caught the telephone ring from the bottom of the garden where she was watering some pot plants. Damn. She'd forgotten to switch on the answerphone. Robin would be cross. That would be him saying when to pick him up.

She dropped the watering can and began the dash back to the house. She reached the door, opened it and put her foot on the doorstep. It gave way beneath her, leaving grassy, muddy evidence of her slide on the metal strip. As she crashed down, she automatically flung out her right arm. It smashed onto the unyielding tiles, causing her to yelp with pain.

Miraculously, when she struggled to the phone, it was still ringing. That was not like Robin; he usually gave up after the fifth ring.

'Hello, Mr Furness here,' said a voice so clear it could have been in the same room. That had her confused. Good heavens, Mr Furness!

'Everything all right?'

'Oh, yes,' she panted. 'Everything's fine, fine.' Desperately she tried to gather her thoughts to remember the things she wanted to ask him. She gained time and breath by a polite, 'How is your trip going?'

'Oh it's great, great. Marvellous weather. Friendly natives,' he laughed.

'Where are you now?'

'Just below Cairns, heading south. That's Queensland. Done the Great Barrier Reef and all that.'

'How wonderful.'

'It was. It was.'

The numbness in her wrist was beginning to wear off to be replaced by an ominous dull pain. 'There was one thing, Mr Furness. I had a bit of trouble with the door of the little spare room upstairs.' Even as she said it, she knew it sounded a trivial problem with which to be spanning the globe. 'Er – I thought it was locked – and, er, I was worried about security,' she finished lamely.

'Is it OK now?'

'Oh yes, fine.'

'Good. It was always a bit stiff. I meant to put a bit of oil on it.' He paused. 'Anything else?' She could hear a woman's voice in the background telling him to hurry up.

'Yes, Linda has gone missing and the police know she used to do a bit of cleaning here—'

'Missing? Run away from home, d'you mean?'

'Well, they think it might be more serious than that. There's been a murder locally.'

'Good heavens!' He sounded genuinely surprised. 'Whatever next? And they think something like that might have happened to Linda?'

'Well, they're not sure. It's possible.'

'Well, my dear, I couldn't be much help, I'm afraid. I never had much to do with her. My wife's department, you understand.'

Oh, she did understand. That, 'my dear', and 'wife's department'. Both dead giveaways of the patronizing old rather than the new man who might at least pretend respect. His wife! of course. His wife!

'Oh yes, that's the other thing, Mr Furness. Your wife called in.'

'Good grief! What did *she* want?' He did not sound pleased.

'To collect some of her property.'

'What property?' The voice was sharper now.

'Oh, just personal things like her passport and driving licence.'

'Huh. The stupid woman left those, did she?'

'I did check her identity before I allowed her to take them. I hope that's OK?'

'Oh, I suppose so.'

Oh, did he? Suddenly Jenny was cross that she had been put in such a position. Her wrist was throbbing now.

'Actually, Mr Furness, I was under the impression that it was your wife who was with you. I must say, the whole thing took me by surprise and I—'

'Sorry, what was that?'

'I said, according to your booking it was Mr and Mrs Furness who were hiring me and—'

'I can't hear you. The line seems to be breaking up.'

It sounded fine to Jenny.

'I can hear *you*. As I said, according to the booking—'

'What? What?'

'Oh, never mind. But,' she shouted, 'the police would like to speak to you about—'

The line had gone dead.

A knock on the kitchen door made her jump out of her skin. It opened to reveal David's cheerful face.

It was a hot day for spring and David had his shirt off as he lopped unruly branches from scraggy bushes. The effect was

109

trim but somewhat shorn-looking, like a poodle after its new summer cut. He was not heavily tanned, she noticed, his skin being a more golden as were the dusting of hairs on his chest. His shoulders were good, broad but not hefty. She didn't like beefy men. David's chest was well-proportioned, his waist and hips narrow and his bottom neat. She noticed all these things quite disinterestedly, she told herself. Being of an artistic bent, satisfactory proportions tended to please her and there was no doubt David's proportions were satisfactory.

He saw her looking and waved. She waved back in an abstracted manner as though she had really been contemplating the view. She tried to force herself back to her painting, but her mind kept drifting in pleasurable anticipation towards their regular, post-gardening chat which, nowadays, was always followed by a short painting lesson.

Was she playing with fire? That's what Aden Bullen had told her. She'd given him the come on, he'd said. Then, when he'd seen that that excuse was not working, he was all contrition and terrible guilt. He'd been driven mad by desire for her. It was the drink. He was mortified by what had happened. He even cried.

'You bastard – that won't save you!' she'd screamed.

That was when he had got really nasty and an ugly defiance had set in. Who would believe she wasn't willing? he'd spat. Alone in the house with him. Leaving the bathroom door unlocked while she had a shower. 'When I tell them how you invited me in, asked me to soap you down and service you meanwhile. Trust me,' he had laughed, 'you don't stand a chance.'

But this was different. David and she had been alone many times without any move on his part. True, there was intimacy in a private painting lesson, the occasional necessary touching of hands in guidance and the brushing of heads as she leaned over his work created a certain electricity. But he never made a move on her. Indeed, she felt he strived to remain deter- minedly controlled and serious in his pursuit of artistic perfection. She appreciated that. It made her feel more secure in his presence and it was a long time since that had happened with a stranger. In any case, he had so much to lose in a job like his.

The phone interrupted her reverie.

'DS Bridgeman here,' was the brisk introduction when she picked up the receiver. 'I got your message that Furness has been in touch.'

'Yes, but only briefly and—'

'You got his forwarding address and phone number, I hope?'

'No, I—'

'Oh damn!'

'I tried to, but the line went dead.'

'Didn't you ask him where he was?'

'Yes, of course!' Jenny did not like the man's tone. She was not one of his underlings. 'He said he was in Queensland, going south from Cairns.'

'You told him we wanted to speak to him?'

'Yes, of course! He said it would be a waste of time, because his wife always dealt with domestic matters.'

'That's not the point!'

'I know what the point is, Sergeant!' I can be peremptory too, she thought. She'd imagined Bridgeman was a nice, caring guy and. . . .

'Sorry, had a bad day.'

'Haven't we all.' He couldn't keep pulling that one, she thought crossly.

'Why, what's happened?'

'Oh, nothing of interest to the police!' Suddenly she felt sorry for him. 'I did ask him about the door.'

'What door?'

David popped into the room, waved his hand and mouthed, 'Goodbye'.

Jenny gestured for him to stay but he shook his head. 'Sorry, can't.' He was gone. Jenny was about to run after him when an insistent voice said, 'What door?'

'The one I thought was locked, but wasn't.' She was ridiculously disappointed. No lovely chat, no lesson, no excitement. The fun had gone out of the day.

'You had time to discuss domestic matters like that – but not to get his forwarding number?' He sounded incredulous.

'How was I to know the line would go dead!' She was furious now.

'Sorry, sorry.'

'So you should be. He said, should you be in the slightest bit interested, that the door had always been stiff and he had meant to oil it before he left.' Really, if a woman had behaved so petulantly, she would have been called menopausal.

'Right.' He paused. 'Are you still out there on your own?'

'I am now,' she exclaimed. 'Thanks to your phonecall.'

'Well, you shouldn't be,' he insisted.

She hung up.

'Sure, I do a bit of the buff stuff,' grinned Jake Runsmith. 'Pays well, dunnit?'

'I don't know,' said Carol. 'You tell me.'

'Well, it does, if you get it right.'

'And you do?'

'Most times.' He was using a puffer brush on his camera lens as he spoke. 'Mind you,' he said looking up. 'it's not so easy as the happy-snappies seem to think. In fact, it's damned hard,' he added in an injured manner. 'But most of them just want to get their rocks off with a starkers babe, don't they?'

'And you don't?'

'Do me a favour.' He opened the back of the Nikon and peered inside. 'I'm too busy getting the flesh tones right, aren't I? Hiding goose bumps an' ugly creases and all that. Keeping the babe sweet. . . . Don't have no time to get no hard on.' He blew squirts of air around the inside of the camera. 'Getting rid of the bits of fluff.' he explained and grinned lewdly. He was a seedy, scraggy-looking man in a tight, grubby, black T-shirt and black jeans which made him look like a pipe cleaner. She could have insisted he gave her his full attention, but she reckoned if she kept it casual she'd prise more out of him as well as getting a better measure of him. Amazing how much that disarmed people.

'Do you do portraits?'

Now that surprised him.

'Yeah,' he nodded. 'Do a bit of everything don't I? When I've got the time, of course.'

'What sort of people?'

'What d'you mean?' he said cagily. He was gently polishing his lens with a small, yellow cloth.

'Children? Families? Young women?'

His head shot up. 'Ah, I get it. I don't do no buff stuff with young girls if that's what you're getting at! Too bloody dodgy.'

'I wasn't talking about nudes, I was talking about straightforward portraits of young women – with their clothes on.'

He was confused. 'Sure, if I'm asked. Why not?'

Carol decided to take a chance.

'Actually, I'd like your help.' She brought out the pictures of Linda and Cynthia. 'I've been told that you sometimes use double catch lights and, frankly, I'm a bit out of my depth here, so bear with me. I wondered whether these might be yours. If not, whose do you think they might be?'

He seemed more confused now, so said nothing. He accepted the prints and studied them warily. It was a while before he said anything. Was it her imagination, or was his hand shaking?

'Not mine,' he said finally.

'You're not certain?'

'No, 'course I'm not absolutely blinkin' certain. Look, I've taken hundreds over the years, haven't I? Don't recognize these, but can't swear on my mother's life that they're not mine. But I don't *think* they are. Unless they're from way back.'

Now there's hedging your bets, Carol thought.

'Well can you suggest someone else?'

He shook his head. 'Could be anyone. No copyright on double catch lights, is there?'

Carol just looked at him and allowed the silence to grow deafening. Nervous people couldn't stand a noisy silence.

'It's them girls, isn't it?' he said eventually, and with some resentment. 'Them missing girls.'

'Yes.'

'Why should I know anything about them?'

13

Rolls was furious. 'You've been checking up on me, Sergeant!' he exclaimed. 'How dare you!'

Ah, so that was why he had suddenly appeared in the front office demanding an interview. Bridgeman had suspected that might be the reason. His friend Harry would have been ultra-careful with his enquiries on Bridgeman's behalf, but he knew that the legal world is a small and very self-protective one.

'You have a murder and two girls missing in suspect circumstances. You appear to have got nowhere in pursuance of these serious matters' – Rolls paused dramatically – 'and you see fit to waste your time checking up on me, a Queen's Counsel.'

I'll be speaking to your chief constable, comes next, thought Bridgeman.

'This is not the last you are going to hear about this,' Rolls threatened. 'I shall be taking it further!'

Oh well, a variation on a theme. Bridgeman sat and waited until the man stopped fuming and began to calm down before saying, slowly and very deliberately, 'Mr Rolls, surely you expected me to make enquiries about you?'

'Yes, but—'

'Correct me if I am wrong,' he rapped out, 'but wouldn't you be the first to complain, accuse us of "dereliction of duty", if we did not "examine every possibility"?'

He was flinging Rolls's own words back at him and even imitating his unpleasant courtroom manner. For once, Rolls appeared uncertain how to react. Bridgeman held on to the initiative by continuing.

'You know as well as I do that we must always look close to home first and that stepfathers are particularly suspect. Particularly stepfathers who have not revealed themselves as such!' Bridgeman was on self-destruct again and did not trouble to conceal his anger. 'You would not, I'm sure,' he went on acidly, 'want the investigation to be carried out differently, just because you are a barrister? And you are not, I hope, attempting to intimidate me, or prevent me from doing my duty?' He paused before giving the man a sop to his dignity, which was more than he had given. 'I'm certain that is not the case, sir. But I am sure you will understand that it would look very odd, suspicious even, if it *were*.'

During his tirade, Rolls had just stared at him, bemused but his changing expression indicated that Bridgeman was hitting home. It was a good feeling.

'Of course, of course, Sergeant,' he conceded, almost placatingly. 'But if you wanted to know something about me, why go behind my back? Why—?'

'Be realistic!' Bridgeman said, losing his patience. 'Would you be likely to tell me if there had been any suggestion of impropriety in your past?' Rolls tried to break in but Bridgeman, having grasped some of the power that this man enjoyed wielding, was not about to allow him. 'Of course I went behind your back! We go behind everybody's back. It's called making enquiries! What do you want us to do? Put out banners, for heaven's sake!' He paused, then back-pedalled just a little. 'I understand how distressed you are, sir, but we are doing everything we can to find your stepdaughter *and* a murderer and the sooner we can eliminate you as one of many possible suspects, the happier we shall be.'

Sod it, thought Bridgeman, I can always run a pub.

Rolls smoothed down his silver-flecked hair and tried to speak again, but Bridgeman held up his hand. 'Just let me finish; I am very busy.' He paused deliberately. 'It may be of some

116

comfort to you to know that I have discovered nothing so far which might point the finger at *you*, but nothing that would exonerate you, either. Since you are here, and have suggested I consult you, it might be helpful if you would fill in more details of your background and suggest contacts which will help verify what you tell us. They will be approached most tactfully and I'm sure that, like you, they will understand the necessity for such routine enquiries.'

Bridgeman felt he had never held the stage for so long without a break. Rolls was accustomed to doing so and knew full well how such a steamrolling technique gave one the upper hand. With him, however, it involved treating suppositions as facts, and those dodgy facts as accusations, then blocking off any objections before the opposition had time to voice them. At least, Bridgeman hadn't uttered the grossly unfair caveat, 'Answer the question: yes or no.'

To Bridgeman's surprise, the urbane barrister just looked at him, smiled slightly and murmured, 'You're absolutely right, Officer. Excellent mitigating speech. Now, what is it you would like to know?'

As it turned out, what Rolls told him didn't add up to much more than what he already knew. Somehow, they wandered way back into the man's early history. Parents hanging on to the edges of lower-middle-class life in Yorkshire. Father in local government, mother a district nurse. Only son showed promise, went to local grammar school, on to university to study law before qualifying and becoming a junior in a small chambers in Gray's Inn. Called to the Bar fifteen years ago. One surprise was that Rolls's father had committed suicide when his son was twenty-four. When Bridgeman gently probed the possible reasons, Rolls shrugged.

'Balance of the mind disturbed was the verdict. My theory was that he had been depressed for many years but was waiting until I had established myself before ending his misery.' He inclined his head and made a rueful moue. 'He was a bit of a manic depressive, I realize now.'

117

'I'm sorry, that must have been hard to live with.'

'Oh, as a child you just tend to accept these things as normal, don't you? Fortunately, my mother was strong and coped cheerfully and encouraged me.' He paused. 'You sometimes wonder, don't you? If she had not been so strong, he might have not felt so useless and unhappy.'

Bridgeman nodded. 'It was the opposite way around with mine,' he admitted.

'There's no way of telling what either of them would have been like without the other, is there?' Rolls smiled slightly in a comradely fashion. 'I suppose it's useless to speculate.'

The man was starting to sound almost human. But was this just another ploy? A deliberate distraction maybe? He would look back at the Yorkshire newspapers for the period when Rolls was growing up – for unsolved sex attacks or murders. The man was handsome, and while middle-age urbanity suited him, he had probably been extremely presentable in his youth. Young sex offenders did tend to be on the spotty and unattractive side – but not always.

Rolls's first marriage had failed after two years. 'We were young and I was working hard to establish myself.' Her name was Marjorie Beaton and he had no idea of her present whereabouts. He added, 'We've lost touch completely.'

As for Cynthia's real father, Edward Barton, relations were 'amicable'. He had a new young family and was able only to keep in intermittent contact. Bridgeman had already been in touch with Barton and judged him not to be in the running as a suspect, or as a provider of much useful information. One thing was certain, Rolls became emotional when he spoke about the girl. Genuine parental concern? Fear? Or something more?

As they worked their way forward through his life, Bridgeman noticed that Rolls omitted to mention the two-year gap which their own enquiries had uncovered. He let it go for now. With a slippery character, it was best to keep some ammunition in reserve. Could be the gap was merely the youthful 'year out' syndrome but, in Rolls's case, coming a bit later and stretching to two years. One odd thing. It had come between his qualifying and joining chambers. A strangely long time when starting out on a career in which networking, contacts and a high profile was so important?

Rolls had met with his present wife, the elegant Clara, at a chambers party 'celebrating a big corporate win', confided Bridgeman's new friend. 'She is the sister of a colleague and we just clicked straight away.' He smiled at the memory. 'Came at a good time for me. I was beginning to feel lonely.' Another claim to vulnerability. Bridgeman felt almost churlish at his own cynicism. Almost. He nodded and opened his mouth to speak.

'And, no, Sergeant, I did not at that time know that Clara had a teenage daughter.'

Bridgeman said nothing but thought that her brother, 'the colleague', might have mentioned it?

Rolls read his mind. 'He wasn't a close colleague. He was new to chambers.' He paused and grinned. 'Charlie is a bit of a prat, actually. I was amazed when this ravishing sister materialized.'

'So when did you get to meet Cynthia?'

'After I'd been out with Clara what, five or six times? She was going down to her school for visiting day and asked if I'd like to come along. Bit of a test, I suppose, to see if I really was committed.'

'And you were?'

'I certainly was. And, as an added bonus, the daughter was utterly charming. I'd been dreading it, of course. But, as with her mother, we seemed to hit it off. No problem. I became very fond of her, very quickly. Surprised even me. I never saw myself as paternal.' He paused, suddenly looking a good deal older than his forty-something years. 'It seemed all too perfect to be true. And it was . . . until now.'

They went on to discuss Cynthia yet again, in case some other clue might come to light.

'Well, Mr Rolls, thank you very much for your co-operation,' Bridgeman concluded at last, adding, 'There's just a couple of things I'd like you to ask Mrs Rolls. Firstly, did Cynthia ever wear underclothes like this, and the same question regarding a certain nail varnish?'

'Of course, Officer, of course.' He paused. 'My reading is that the murder victim was wearing these things.'

Bridgeman just looked at him and said nothing.

It was clearly going to be a difficult interview. Bridgeman felt sorry for the young couple, who were crouching close together on a settee covered in what looked like bleached sacking. Their house, a Victorian semi, was decorated and furnished in an extremely odd combination of styles. The kitchen, which he had glimpsed through the hall door on his way in, was like something out of a violent nightmare – all strong red, mauves and purples. In contrast, the hall and the lounge where they were sitting, was starkly minimalist and pale. Anaemic cream and weak-tea beige upholstery on cane seating abutted with chrome and glass side tables. He guessed they were in the process of redecorating after previous occupiers and he wondered which of the two styles was their taste – probably the latter. Small wonder Avril Scanscombe had found it difficult to settle in here, coming as she did from a shabby but cosy semi-d. on the Rainby Estate.

Mrs Bagnall, 'Janey', was insubstantial and wispy. Her snub nose, rabbity mouth and disappearing chin put Bridgeman in mind of Lucy, the nervous hamster he'd had as a child. You'd never describe her as attractive, he decided, even when she wasn't distressed. But he could see she had a certain waiflike appeal – if you like that sort of thing. He didn't.

'She'd never been away from home before, which, of course, wasn't our fault,' Janey said, 'and she had no other friends around here.' She began crying again. Her husband, who had been holding her hand, now released it to put a protective arm around her.

'It wasn't your fault, love,' he said. 'She'd just had little Arthur,' he explained to Bridgeman. 'Avril was supposed to help her, but didn't really. Then she refused to eat what we ate.'

'You're vegetarians?' Bridgeman guessed.

She nodded. 'Avril said she gave that sort of food to her pet rabbit,' Janey sniffed, 'and I got a bit cross. I thought everyone knew about vegetarianism these days, even down there in Birchfield.'

Bridgeman shook his head sadly. 'People get stuck in their ways, don't they?' he murmured comfortingly.

'Lots of young girls are supposed to be into it these days, aren't they?' she complained again. She might be sorry about Avril's death but, despite her tearful protestations, was not about to shoulder any of the blame for the girl's sudden departure.

Bridgeman refrained from pointing out that such a recently bereaved girl might have needed patient handling and instead, paused for a decent length of time, then said, 'So that was it, really? Just normal domestic upsets and misunderstandings?'

They both nodded dumbly. The husband, Bridgeman decided, was more physically appealing than the wife. But he was also coarser: sturdily built with rather wild, thick, black hair, sharp, black eyes and bulky, bricklayer hands.

'I'm away a lot on site, so that made it more difficult for Janey.'

'You're a builder?' murmured Bridgeman politely.

The man shook his head. 'No, I'm an architect.'

Well, how wrong can you be, thought Bridgeman. There was clearly more to this man than met the eye.

The hamster-like Janey and her beefy, but obviously reasonably intelligent husband, could not think of anywhere Avril could have fled to or any person she might have gone with. She had made no new friends while with them, they asserted. They did know that she had a girlfriend back in Birchfield, but they could neither recall her name nor her whereabouts. They would give it some thought, they promised. No, her name was not Linda. At least they didn't think so.

'So what was Avril like – to look at, I mean?' he asked suddenly. 'The general impression she gave, I mean?'

121

There was a short silence during which Bridgeman sensed the man holding back.

'Attractive,' said the wife.

14

'I need to speak to the husband on his own,' Bridgeman said down the phone.

'You think something was going on there?' asked Glass.

'Dunno. There's a bit of tension, definitely. But that's understandable, I suppose.'

'How about the neighbours?'

'Three wise monkeys, basically. Saw the girl about a bit, sometimes with the pram. But most of them are out all day and don't know the Bagnalls very well anyway, them being new there. I might get something from the old dear next door but she's away for the weekend.'

'No one saw Avril leave?'

'Nope. That's the tricky one.'

'Seems a bit odd that they've no idea where she may have gone. You want to get a search warrant?'

'Not yet, I don't think.'

'So, when are you seeing the husband?'

'He's coming into the nick tomorrow to give a blood sample – elimination purposes he's been told. But I don't think I'll hang about. It's my feeling it would be better to let him stew a little first. I'll talk to him when I come back to see the old dear, if that's all right.'

'Yes. Fine.' He paused. 'Hope you're right.'

'Me too.'

It had happened again. David had come to do the garden and they had worked companionably all morning, if not side by side, at least within hailing distance of each other. She was on the patio, capturing the contrasts of a weathered stone urn and its cargo of glistening white hyacinths, he going to and fro doing some general tidying up, planting out, snipping and mulching.

When he passed her, he had exchanged the odd word or smile now and then, stopping to glance at the work in progress and teasingly offer advice.

'A bit of Payne's gray needed there', he'd said, pointing to the shadow side of the pot, and, 'that needs knocking back a bit', of some, as yet, too prominent background.

Then, after all this warmth and comradeship, he had not stopped for coffee, chat, or his painting lesson. She couldn't understand. As twelve o'clock had neared, she had put her brushes down and gone to put on the coffee and get out the biscuits – at a critical moment when she would have been better employed getting her darks in and capturing those shadows before the light changed too much. The break in concentration would be compensated for by his smile of pleasure as the wonderful aroma greeted him as he opened the kitchen door.

Come twelve, he had popped his head around the door, said, 'All done. See you next week. Bye,' given a wave and left.

By the time she had recovered her power of speech he had reached his van. In retrospect, it was rather humiliating, pathetic perhaps, how she had run after him, saying, 'Aren't you staying for a coffee? It's on – won't take a minute.'

'Sorry,' he'd replied casually. 'Schedule too tight today,' and was gone. But he'd had tight schedules before and he had to drink sometime!

She was ridiculously disappointed again. What was wrong? Had he imagined she was getting too interested in him and backed off for safety's sake? But she'd made it plain she was merely being friendly. Maybe that was it? He'd felt snubbed in some way? Ever since Aden Bullen's attack she seemed to have lost the code for male/female friendship. He had ruined so much for her, and not just her. Oh, if only it had ended there, on the bathroom floor with him sneering down at her.

She'd still been determined to fight back, been determined to report him to the police despite his jibes that the jury would see her actions as invitation and see she had been a willing party. But when he had pointed out what it would do to her beloved brother Martin's career chances she had been undone. If only she had done the right thing.

Eddie Bates, the burly truck driver, stood grinning shyly at Jenny. His substantial frame.was encased in green dungarees. On his large head he wore a dark-green woolly hat pulled low over his forehead. In his huge hands, he grasped a tiny bunch of field poppies and white Michaelmas daisies.

'They was in a field by the lay-by when I picked up one of the girls and I thought' – he cleared his throat – 'I thought you might like them to paint.' He thrust the posy towards her.

'Oh, how right you were, Eddie,' she enthused, smiling warmly at him as she accepted them. 'Poppies are one of my favourite flowers. They're so vibrant and cheerful, but have such a simplicity about them.' She began filling another vase with water. 'You've got to be quick with poppies, they drop so soon.'

He grinned at her, pleased.

'In fact,' she said, surveying her floral arrangement, 'I think I might adjust this a little.' She whipped some rather-past-their-best tulips from a vase and replaced them with the dancing scarlet and white field flowers. 'This will be a good exercise for you all. Red is tricky – particularly when you try to darken it without killing it. Thank you, Eddie.'

The lumbering fellow blushed then turned away and wandered over to the sink to select a water container from the seedy selection of jam pots, jars and jugs lining the draining board.

Almost a full house this evening, Jenny noticed, with some satisfaction. The neat and professional Mrs Petty was already well into her preparatory thumbnail sketches prior to launching on her picture proper. Georgina and Helen, the two escapee housewives, had greeted everyone, had a giggly little chat with each other and were now settling down. Mrs Hedges, who of course had looked indignant at the last minute substitution of the tulips by the poppies, was still tutting and glancing expectantly at Jenny, awaiting the constant, individual, one-to-one tuition she felt her due. She made a big show of pulling her topcoat around her and shivering ostentatiously. 'This *room* – why does it always have to be *so cold!*'

Jenny longed to say, 'Well, if you dressed for it properly you silly cow, you wouldn't be shivering. You've been coming here long enough to know better than wear a silk shirt!'

Instead, she murmured, 'Would you like to borrow my woolly, Mrs Hedges?'

Needless to say, Mrs Hedges preferred to suffer, but not in silence, and to allow her gaunt frame several more meaningful judders.

Ellie Prinks had already done her usual stalking around the set-piece selecting the best possible angle worthy of a semi-professional artist such as she.

'Hmm,' she murmured eventually. 'Bit of an obvious colour, red, don't you think?'

'They're flowers!' Jenny longed to yell at her. 'They come in all colours!' Instead, she said, 'I'm sure you'll bring your usual flair to the subject,' which caused the vain young woman to preen unpleasantly, and the two elderly Bristow sisters to exchange knowing glances before starting on one of their own amazing duo painting exercises.

These two actually painted in unison, on the same painting, a procedure which had at first astonished Jenny. But when she saw how it seemed to work for them, saw no reason to object. They started, as they always did, with a short, whispered conference. Then the stout Hilda set about laying a light background wash while little Emily began mixing and testing out various colours for the next stage.

So, nine in all of her protégés out of a possible ten. Only one missing. Well, two if you counted David. She'd had one eye on the door ever since she came into the empty classroom, hoping, but not really expecting him. He hadn't showed up for the last two lessons and, after his copping out of their morning chats recently, she did not realistically expect an appearance now.

A hush descended on the group as they became engrossed, the only sound being the murmur of Jenny's voice as she placated and advised Mrs Hedges. She ended up with a, 'Right, you're on your own, now,' and got up and walked away. She was aware the woman would be furious at such abandonment, but there was only so much nonsense she could take.

It was ridiculous how depressed she felt by the non-appearance of David. He was nothing to her really. They shared this love of flowers and she saw him as a promising, if not very patient, student. Their association was companionable, that was all. She had just decided to wipe him out of her mind for ever when he arrived.

'Hi,' he grinned, as sanguine and chirpy as ever. He was looking very spruce in jeans and a denim jacket over a cherry-red T-shirt and his hair was held back by the leather thong. 'All well at it already, I see.'

'Hello,' Jenny endeavoured to be as nonchalant as he, but she felt a rosy blush rising from her neck. To hide her confusion she casually indicated the set-up. 'Tonight's subject,' her voice came out quite crisply. 'Better find yourself a seat.' She turned away to answer Mrs Hedges' peremptory beckonings, despite having decided to let her go to hell.

David, unfazed, acknowledged all the nods of welcome from the other pupils and pretended not to notice the rolling of eyes by the escapee housewives at the sight of an attractive man in their midst.

Once settled, he looked expectantly at Jenny, raised his eyebrows and pointed from the still-life with flowers to his blank sheet of watercolour paper and back again. She couldn't help laughing.

'I didn't expect to see you tonight,' she said, as she sat down beside him. 'I thought your artistic muse must have deserted you.'

'Oh, no,' he said, 'it's just that. . . .' He stopped.

'It's just that, what?' she exclaimed lightly.

'Well, I feel a bit out of my depth here. The others are so much more experienced than me.'

'Good grief! It's not a competition!' She smacked his wrist. 'I hate that attitude.'

'Oops, sorry.'

'You proceed at your own pace. You know that. The only person you're in competition with is yourself!'

'Huh. Very philosophical. I'll work that one out later.'

She looked skywards imploringly. 'Of course, they're further ahead than you. They've been doing it longer!'

He pulled at his pony-tail. 'Sure, I know that. But when I'm sat down like this I don't really know where to start. I need some more basic lessons.'

What a cheek. Hadn't she been giving him basic private lessons back at the house?

'Well, sign on for a beginner's class,' she snapped.

'Rather not. I'd rather you taught me.'

'I *was* teaching you. Indeed, giving you private tuition. But you haven't been staying on after your work.'

He shook his head. 'Can't stay in the daytime any more. Too many commitments.'

'Well, why not come around in the evening?'

He laughed. 'And what would your husband think about that?'

'Robin's not my husband. Anyway, nothing. Why should he? You're a pupil. Besides, half the time he's not back until around midnight these days.'

'Oh, I see.' He looked knowing.

'No you don't.'

'OK. When would you like me to come?'

'Tomorrow night?'

She realized she'd said it too quickly.

15

His trip was proving more fruitful than he'd expected.

'Oh yes,' said the Bagnalls' neighbour, back from her weekend away, 'I remember Avril very well. A smiley girl – except the smiles grew more strained the longer she stayed next door.'

She was a loquacious woman with a conspiratorial manner, but not mischievous in Bridgeman's opinion. They were sitting in her trinket-filled living-room over cups of Earl Grey tea.

'She used to chat to me over the fence, longing for a bit of sensible company.' She nodded towards the Bagnall house and lowered her voice. 'Bit odd that one, if you ask me.'

'Did Avril get on with him all right, d'you think?'

'Oh yes, I think so.' She leaned closer. 'But if you're thinking there might have been some hanky-panky you'd be wrong.' She shook her silvery head. 'He's only concerned about his little wifey.'

'Right,' said Bridgeman, thinking if I stay here long enough she'll have the case solved for me.

'That was the trouble if you ask me. They were like two broody chickens over that baby. Only had eyes for each other and it. Avril was like a cuckoo in the nest. Close is nice, I know, but that's weird.'

'So hanky-panky is out according to my guru,' he informed Carol later. 'And I think she's right.'

'Hmm. Wouldn't be so sure,' she warned. 'Just because he's

129

obsessional about one woman doesn't mean he won't invite another to share his nest. Seen those sort of blokes before. Creepily close to his wife so you feel safe but then he makes a pass at you just the same.'

'I must bow to your superior knowledge.'

'I've told you before—'

'Men are weird.'

'Right. And they get nasty when they are turned down.' She looked thoughtful. 'There is another possible scenario.'

'She didn't turn him down and the wife did the deed.'

'Well that's another one, but I was thinking what if she was being difficult with the beloved Janey and he just lost his rag.'

'And meanwhile deposited two different types of sperm on the body.'

'Oh, forgot about that.'

'You're losing it, girl.'

She wished she was, with him.

'What did *he* say by the way?'

'Same as before really. Stressing how hard it had all been for Saint Janey and how good she'd been about it. Didn't deny there had been raised voices on the night before she left.'

'He wasn't worried about talking to you?'

'No. Funny thing. He came to me. Stopped me as I was coming out of the old dear's place wanting to make sure I'd got everything I wanted. Janey was out at her mother's so we had a long chat – which left me no wiser really.'

'What I can't understand,' Carol had said to Bridgeman after they had learned that Linda Blackstone and Avril had been mates, 'is why Linda's mum did not recognize the description of Avril or the artist's impression?'

'Well, all young girls look alike these days, don't they?' he had replied, causing Carol to look at him and exclaim, 'Blimey, you *are* jaded!'

'No, come on. They all wear their hair long and straight and wear the same sort of clothes. . . .'

130

'But the body was almost naked.'

He had just shrugged. 'Well, I dunno.'

Now, Carol put the question to Linda's mum. She had already told them that Linda and Avril had known each other quite well but had not been bosom pals, Avril being 'a bit more serious' than her daughter.

Carol recognized this as parent-speak for the fact that Avril had probably been cleverer than Linda. What it boiled down to was that the pair had gone 'to look at the shops together now and then', to the occasional disco, and once or twice Avril had taken Linda to the animal rescue centre. 'But she didn't like that much 'cos of the messes the animals made. She didn't want to do no cleaning out, like Avril did.'

'We were surprised,' said Carol, tactfully avoiding any hint of criticism, 'that you didn't recognize the artist's drawing of the girl found in the woods.'

Mrs Blackstone's expression froze for a moment. She stared at Carol, her lips moving but no sound coming out. Then she blushed and whispered, 'I never looked at it. Couldn't bear to. I was so relieved when I heard the description and knew it couldn't be Linda and. . . .' She tailed off. She shrugged and looked guilty. 'I suppose I should have.'

Bridgeman shook his head. 'No, not necessarily. It's quite understandable.'

'Will you look at it now?' Carol asked quickly.

Mrs Blackstone frowned and looked puzzled. 'What good. . . ? I mean, I thought you knew. . . .'

'Oh we do. We are certain it's Avril. No question. But we want to know why other people didn't recognize it as her.'

'Oh, right.' She pushed her hair back behind her ears and began glancing about her nervously, as if for help. 'You know it's been a long time since I saw Avril – an' then I didn't see her that often when she was living in Birchfield – what with me going out to work, an' all.'

'*Anything* you tell us could be of help,' Carol assured her. 'Don't worry, it's not gruesome.'

131

Mrs Blackstone nodded and stretched out her hand to take the print. When she finally steeled herself to look at it, she seemed relieved. 'Well, it don't look like her, does it?' she asked. 'That's why no one could tell.'

'Really?' Carol was startled. Her sister had recognized her. 'Not at all?' she encouraged.

'Well, only a bit.'

Carol and Bridgeman waited while the older woman continued to gaze perplexedly at the drawing of a young girl who had been so cruelly deprived of her life before it had really begun.

Finally, she took a deep breath and said: 'This girl's a lot thinner and her hair's different. Avril's was short and spiky when I knew her and, I dunno. . . .' She frowned at the picture then held up her hand. 'I know. That's it. She's not smiling.'

Carol tried not to react to this odd statement about a dead girl not smiling, confining herself to murmuring, 'But you did say she was a "serious" girl?'

'Oh, yeh. Yeh, she was. In what she liked and everything. But she was always smiling.' Suddenly she smiled herself, warming to her theme in her relief at being able to put her finger on the reason why it didn't look like Avril. 'I used to call her Smiler!' she said in triumph. Then the awful incongruity hit her and she began to cry. ' 'Course, she wouldn't be smiling in the picture, would she?' she exclaimed bitterly. 'She's dead! Like my Linda! Stone dead!'

Carol leaned across the kitchen table and patted and stroked the woman's head as she sobbed into her cupped hands. 'Thanks, you've been a big help. Don't get up, we'll let ourselves out.'

At first sight, the Springfield Park Animal Rescue Centre was rather more sordid than they had expected. Sadly lacking were the pristine standards of the RSPCA and the PDSA as seen on television. Situated at the end of a short lane two and a half miles west of Birchfield, it was within sight and and sound of the M1 and was, as far as Carol could see, not a park at all. A large green notice-board at the top of the lane had announced its presence and explained that the charity was 'Supported entirely by voluntary donations'. A smaller, handwritten notice in the window of the large, old, brick-built farmhouse stated that visitors were welcome and donations appreciated. But the discordant cacophony of barks coming from beyond a high, green, side door had already assured them they had the right place.

Carol and Bridgeman looked at the peeling paint and rickety hinges, then at each other. Was this one of those cowboy outfits battening on to poor strays, or run by oddballs who might be willing, but too woolly-minded, to organize it properly?

Inside, a middle-aged woman with wispy hair and a smiling face was barricaded behind a long reception counter displaying various animal-related gifts and leaflets describing the work of the charity.

'Hello. I'm Mrs Blair, the manager,' she said. 'Would you like to have a look around?'

'Well, yes, we would,' said Carol and could feel Bridgeman stiffen with surprise. 'Then, we would like to have a word with you, if that's OK?'

'Certainly, my dears. Just go on through. You'll find the kennels directly ahead of you and the cattery is to the right at the end.'

It was all surprisingly casual. Once through the door, Bridgeman looked at Carol with lowered brows and puckered lips. His Inspector Morse, what-the-heck's-this-rubbish-all-about look she called it.

'Two reasons,' she said in response. 'First, it gives us a chance to look around – get an idea of what the place is like, without anyone breathing down our necks. Second, my two monsters are nagging me for a puppy and I've told them I'll think about it. Might as well see what Springfield Park has to offer. Better to rescue if poss, don't you think?'

Bridgeman gazed around the shabby wooden buildings forming the alleyway down to the kennels and sucked his teeth. 'From here?'

'Well, if it's bad they'll be more in need of rescue, won't they?' she retorted.

'And full of disease,' he retorted.

As they approached the kennels the bedlam grew louder. Moreso, when the dogs spotted them, each animal pathetically desperate to attract their attention. Carol was horrified by the concrete floors and walls, the eager, doggie faces pushing against the ugly wire mesh. It looked so basic, so cold and well – just awful. A tiny, one-eyed Yorkshire terrier caught her eye as it waved its right paw in the air, then scampered around in frantic excitement. Next door, a German Shepherd cross had a deafening and melancholy bark, as if warning of impending doom, while its neighbour, a liver-and-cream spaniel, stood up on its hind legs yelping and whimpering trying to reach out towards them. According to the card slotted into a panel on the outside of the cage, she was Marmie, seemingly abandoned, who had been found starving and wandering on nearby farmland.

'Oh, God,' said Carol, 'this is awful. I never thought it would be this bad. I want to take them all home.'

It wasn't the conditions which upset her so much. In fact, she was beginning to realize that the kennel block, although in need of a coat of paint, was perfectly clean and adequate. Each pen had a large piece of sacking for the occupant to lie on, there was water in their bowls and they had obviously been fed. It was the desperation in their eyes that got to her.

'I think I've had enough,' said Bridgeman suddenly. He had been gazing at two greyhounds cowering in the corner, peering upwards with the saddest eyes he had ever seen. Their notices announced they were ex-racers, thrown out when their money-spinning form came to an end.

It turned out that Mrs Blair remembered Avril well. 'She was a lovely, smiling girl.' What's more, she had recognized the artist's impression. 'Well, I thought I did. But the others said it couldn't be her with that hair and everything, so, I'm afraid' – she shrugged and looked embarrassed – 'I accepted their opinion. I did have second thoughts and wondered and was going to ring you, but we had a torrent of admissions and it got pushed to the back of the priorities.'

The others, it turned out, were her husband and two permanent assistants, a married couple, who helped them run the sanctuary. Neither were there at that moment. Carol arranged to see them the next day.

'Any other regular visitors?' asked Bridgeman.

The woman spread her hands. 'Several, just like Avril. You know, animal lovers who walk the dogs and help out around the kennels and catteries.'

'We'd like a list please.'

She looked a bit nonplussed at this. 'I'm not absolutely sure of all their second names and where they all come from. . . .' She tailed off. 'But, all right. I'll try.'

'By tomorrow would be splendid,' said Carol, taking out a five-pound note and slipping it in the collection box. 'We'd really appreciate that.'

Mrs Blair smiled her thanks and nodded dazedly. 'Anything I can do to help catch the killer of that poor child. But I shouldn't think it would be anyone who comes here.'

'Maybe not,' said Bridgeman, 'but they might just know something. We're still building a picture of her, you see.'

'Do you keep getting the feeling that we've missed something?' asked Carol as they drove away up the lane. 'Something jumping out at us that we've failed to focus on?'

Bridgeman looked as his watch. 'I certainly do. I really should have left this one to you. The whole case might have blown wide open while I've been away.'

'You know very well they'd have belled you if there was anything important,' said Carol.

'*If* they knew it was important.'

'Oh, indispensable now, are we?'

'No. But I'm the one who has the overall view. The office manager's job is in the office.'

'Give yourself a break. Like you said, you also need to get the feel of the enquiries out and about.' She patted his hand in motherly fashion. 'It'll be all right, you'll see.'

'Right, Mum,' he laughed, and thought it was a pity he didn't fancy her for more than a friend. She was such a comfort.

Jenny tried on several different casual tops, discarding them one after another. What she wanted was something which made her look good, without it seeming as though she was wearing anything special, or that she had made any particular effort. Finally, she settled for the harebell blue which matched her eyes. It was a little more formal than she had intended, but if she wore it over her scruffiest jeans. . . . Ear-rings to match? No, that really *would* be too much. But maybe a touch of lipstick and blusher? She was looking a little pale. She opened the top drawer of the dresser before realizing it was the wrong one. Her belongings were in the chest of drawers. As she closed the drawer she glimpsed a glint of glassy green, peeping from beneath a coverlet of black velvet.

She opened the drawer again and folded back the velvet to reveal a cornucopia of green jewellery. Some stones were of matt and solid jade, others, glittering and transparent like emeralds. Some, scattered along dramatic, swirling whirlwinds of fine gold wire, others held by weird and wonderful mythical beasts. Oh God! Hadn't the dead girl been wearing a ring with a green stone grasped by some sort of animal?

She cogitated about it then picked up the bedroom phone, rang Birchfield Police Station and asked for Sergeant Bridgeman. He wasn't there. Did she want to speak to anyone else? She thought quickly. One thing she didn't want was her time with David interrupted again. 'No, I'll ring back. Just tell him who called and say I will ring him back.' She looked outside. The light was fading fast making the outhouse shadowy and threatening. Never mind, stop being such a wimp! she chastized herself. You never used to be like this! David would be here soon anyway. She checked her watch. In about thirty-five minutes in fact, but her mood of warm expectation had been rudely crushed by her find.

What the heck did it mean, all this jewellery resembling the ring on the murdered girl? Now calm down, she told herself. Be sensible. It probably means nothing at all. Avril's friend came here to do a bit of cleaning. The woman of the house, whoever she was, had this jewellery, maybe made it, and she gave a ring to Linda. Linda gave it, or lent it to Avril. That's it. That's all. What's so odd about that? But she couldn't shake off a sense of foreboding.

Things still to do. That would help. She applied a little blusher and lipstick to her now even paler face, then dashed downstairs to the kitchen. She took out four home-made scones and placed them on a baking tray near the oven. Warm scones, dripping with whipped cream and topped by dollops of home-made strawberry jam. What could be better? Cream. Oh, damn! She'd forgotten to get the cream! Was everything destined to go wrong that evening? Just like before? Was she mad to be alone in the house with David? Hadn't she learned her lesson?

No! It was not just like before. Then there had been no lead up, no sense of foreboding then and it had not been dark. It had been a lovely, sunny, ordinary day. Besides, wasn't she always on her own when David was here?

Besides, it hadn't been her carelessness which had led to the rape. How was she to know the bathroom lock was dodgy and that Aden Bullen had contrived to be in the house when the others had gone out? It was the decision she had taken afterwards which had been so wrong and for which she would never forgive herself.

Those two other girls need never have suffered had she told. Particularly the fifteen-year-old, Holly Brown, to whom he did such terrible things. That was what had undone her so, her awful guilt. She couldn't forgive herself, even though her lack of action had been for her brother's sake and even though the policewoman comforted her by saying that Aden Bullen was probably right. Supposing the CPS had taken the case to court, which was doubtful, the jury would most likely have believed him, not Jenny. It happened all the time. In earlier cases, rapists would deny all contact, but with the advent of DNA the regular defence had become 'she consented' or even, brazenly, 'she encouraged and even initiated the intercourse'. Jenny was not to blame herself. But she did.

She dragged her mind back to the matter in hand. Remorse was fruitless. Just learn by it. Now, cream. One thing certain, it was too late to dash to the village shop. It may be only two miles away but Pennymead had never taken to late shopping. Freezer. There was usually some in the freezer at most places. No one would mind her snitching a little cream. She could replace it tomorrow. She ran her finger down the meticulous list taped to the door of the kitchen fridge's small freezer compartment. 'Cream:' it said, 'double and single and whipping, outhouse 2 freezer'.

Oh, bugger. There were no keys on the board for outhouse 2. Wait a minute. Hadn't there been some spare keys in the brass vase she emptied and washed to put daffs in?

And there they were. Tagged outhouse 1 and outhouse 2. No problem. Except she now had to go out there in the dark. Stupid, stupid, stupid, she told herself. Cowardy custard. Do you seriously think someone is lurking out there. Just waiting for you to decide to get some cream from the outhouse freezer? Just grab the torch and go. Won't take a minute.

She went. The key fitted and turned. No problem. Groping about she located the light switch. The light was weak and the bulb covered in dust and cobwebs but gave just enough illumination for her purpose, as long as she leaned to one side so as not to get in her own light. The long chest freezer took up much of the floor space but cluttered around it were rusting garden forks and tools, wooden storage boxes, packages and cans which had once held lubricating oil. There was not much room for manoeuvre.

As she tried to lift the heavy lid she leaned backwards trying to avoid getting dust onto her blue top, but managed to brush her sleeve against a long, dusty, upright package, half leaning against the right-hand side of the freezer. Suddenly, she felt terrified. What could be worse? Being out in the open in the dead of night, or trapped inside a small hut like this?

A crackling noise made her stop and listen hard. What was it – that crackling, rustling sound? A mouse? A rat! Imagination? Oh God! The quicker she got on with it, the quicker she would be out of there and safe back inside. 'Just concentrate, woman!' A taped list on the freezer chest lid stated, 'Cream, far right'. But the frost lay so heavy on the contents she couldn't see what was what. She began pushing the packages aside frantically. Then her heart stopped. A pair of eyes were staring up at her! Oh, my God! But it was only the way the ice had formed around two fishes on a dark blue packet. She grasped the edge of the freezer to steady herself. Damn it, David would have to make do with butter. What was wrong with butter? Why was she going to all this trouble? It was ridiculous. *She* was ridiculous.

Furious with herself, she reached up for the freezer lid pulling it down sharply. It caught on the huge package again. She jerked it, angrily. The package began to fall forward and sideways, towards her. She pushed it away, trying to hold it up and push it back at the same time. It felt squishy. She pushed it again, in a panic. It was heavy and unwieldy – and out of control. She couldn't fend it off!

Suddenly, a long split appeared in the plastic wrapping, an overwhelming stench hit her, and a hand, a blackish, rotting hand, thrust itself on to her harebell-blue blouse. Her horror-stricken screams filled the dusty outhouse as she fought to push the ghastly thing off. It fell sideways on to the freezer then toppled on to the floor. Jenny ran, in sheer terror, straight into a dark figure barring her way.

16

She was being shaken. Hands, strong hands gripping her shoulders, short and sharp, back and forth.

'Stop screaming!' a far-off voice was saying. 'Stop screaming!' Then, 'What did you see?' The hands shook her again. 'Tell me what you saw!'

Suddenly, she felt a stinging slap to her left cheek, knocking the breath out of her and making her choke on her screams. Her hand went up to her face as she struggled to get away, coughing and sobbing at the same time.

'It's *me!* Only me!' shouted the voice. A man's voice. Not David. Not Robin. Still holding her shoulders he propelled her forward so that she could see his stocky outline and fair, thinning hair in the dim light from the outhouse, 'It's Sergeant Bridgeman!'

She stared at him then dissolved into torrents of tears. He put his arms around her and, while Carol pushed past them, murmured gently, 'You're all right now. Don't worry. Everything's all right.' He grimaced. 'God, the smell. I think I can guess what you saw in there.'

Carol emerged holding a handkerchief over her mouth, closed the door, fished out her personal radio and began summoning the troops.

'Let's go indoors,' said Bridgeman.

'Well, at least it seems as if we've found one of the missing girls,' murmured Carol, after they'd left Jenny in the hands of a young, uniformed policewoman.

140

Once Glass arrived it was decided that, after photographs and prints had been taken and a thorough inspection made of the outside, the most sensible procedure was to transport the packaged body as it was, in its wrapping. The outhouse was too cramped to allow for further examination *in situ*. The SOCO, photographer, forensics *et al* came out looking green and one young new boy actually threw up over the hyacinth pots on the patio.

'Well, what do you make of all this?' asked Glass.

'Damned if I know,' said Bridgeman. His hair was ruffled and his shirt rumpled and tear-stained with smudges of pale-pink lipstick. 'One thing's certain, though,' he went on, straightening his tie and tucking in his shirt, under the gaze of the immaculate Glass, 'Mr Furness has jumped to the top of the list of our prime suspects. He knew Linda; she came to this house. Could have been some sort of hanky-panky going on. . . .'

'Where's he, then?'

'In Australia. Somewhere between the Great Barrier Reef and Sydney.'

'Oh, very useful.'

'Well, we *think* that's where he is. Who knows? This bloody case is like a Chinese puzzle. Maybe that's just where he would like us to think he is.' His gaze wandered towards the kitchen.

'You can go and see her again in a minute, Sergeant,' murmured Glass with a slight smile. 'Just remind me of all we've got on this Furness, this house and the young woman.'

He told him, beginning with, 'It's all a bit weird. . . .'

'And when did she first notice this ... this parcel?' Glass enquired when Bridgeman had finished.

'Never seen it before. She's never even been in the outhouse before. No reason to.'

Glass frowned, 'So, why did she go in there tonight?'

Bridgeman gave a wry smile. 'She wanted to find some cream from the deep freeze to put with some home-made scones.'

Glass didn't say anything at first, just gazed thoughtfully at his pristine fingernails before flicking an imaginary bit of fluff from his suit. 'Funny thing to have on your own at this time of night – a cream tea? Is she pregnant?'

'No, well, not as far as I know.' Bridgeman reddened slightly and didn't know why. He felt very silly. 'Well, it was a bit earlier then, of course. Early evening.'

Glass waved his hand dismissively. 'Was she expecting visitors?'

'I don't know.' Privately, Bridgeman thought this all a bit academic, given the circumstances. What difference did it make why she went out there? It was what she found and who had the access to put it there, which mattered.

'Is there a regular man?'

'Yes. He's living here too.'

'So, where is he now?'

'In London, job-seeking. At least, that's what he tells her.'

'I see.' Glass grimaced. 'Bit dodgy is he?'

'Dunno, to be honest. Never clapped eyes on him.' Bridgeman looked abashed and shrugged. 'Just being an old cynic.'

'Well, anyway, we'll be putting him under the microscope when he finally does get home. Not a place to leave a woman on her own, is it?'

Bridgeman's feelings exactly.

'Who had access?' asked Glass finally.

'I don't know. But I do know there is a gardener.'

'Right, off you go and ask her.'

A deathly pale Jenny was hunched over the Aga, a blanket wrapped tightly around her, shivering. The first thing she'd done when she'd got in was to dash upstairs and tear off the tainted top. She'd wanted to bathe as well but had been dissuaded.

'It's a good job I called the station to see if there had been any developments,' said Bridgeman. 'When they told me you'd phoned I thought we might as well pop in while passing.'

'Sa-a-a-ved my life,' Jenny stuttered. She wished she could stop sobbing. Why wasn't Robin there? She wanted Robin!

'Not quite,' he laughed gently. 'Your sanity perhaps,' he

added kindly, and was rewarded with a tremulous smile. 'Drink your tea.'

She held the cup with two hands and still couldn't steady it, but just managed to reach her mouth. Where was Robin!

'Some – jewellery . . . I found a pile of jewellery with green stones in it and animal motifs and . . . and I remembered about the ring found on the dead girl's body.'

'Avril,' said Bridgeman. 'Her name's Avril.' He hated victims being referred to as bodies, once they had a name for them.

'I thought you might be interested in the jewellery!' Jenny snapped.

He smiled. 'That's better.'

She glared at him.

'I am, very interested,' he admitted. 'But, the thing is, we're going to have to have a long chat with you and your partner and your agency. In the meantime, just a few of the more pressing questions.'

'All right.' She gave up with the tea and put the cup on the Aga.

'First off, who else has keys to that outhouse?'

'I don't know.'

He looked puzzled.

'There were no keys for it on the board,' she explained. 'Then I remembered some loose keys in a brass vase and it was there.'

'Hasn't that gardener got a set?'

She shook her head. 'No. Well, I shouldn't think so. He always comes to the house for any keys and I've never seen him going into that outhouse.' She thought for a moment then said, 'But that doesn't mean he hasn't been in there. I'm usually busy painting or cooking while he's here so I wouldn't necessarily notice.'

'That's the other thing: we need to speak to him sharpish. What's his name?'

'David.'

Bridgeman waited, pen poised. She blushed. 'I'm afraid that's all I know.' She got out the notes left by Mr Furness and showed him. 'That's all it says, "David, the gardener Monday 12–2 p.m." '

'No surname or address?' Bridgeman was puzzled.

'No. Well he's not a keyholder or emergency contact so there's no need.' He was making her feel foolish not knowing.

'You *should* know for your own security,' he admonished.

'Well, I don't,' she rejoindered, sharply. What business was it of his?

She didn't like his tone. 'I wasn't to know that, was I? No one told me there was a body in the outhouse!' It sounded so melodramatic she couldn't stop a tearful, hysterical laugh rising in her throat.

Bridgeman chuckled too and looked at her admiringly.

'I do know he works at the Singlewood Nursery on the Headington–Louden Road, just south of Pennymead.'

'That's what he told you.'

'Yes.' She hesitated then said, 'And I saw him there.' She blushed.

'Ah. Right.' There was a short silence. 'By the way,' he said eventually, 'my boss wants to know why you wanted cream for the scones. He couldn't picture you sitting here, scoffing them on your own.'

'I wasn't going to,' said Jenny, then stopped.

'Yes?' Bridgeman encouraged.

'Someone was coming for a painting lesson. They were for him,' she said defiantly.

'And that was?' His voice had grown cooler and his pen was poised expectantly again.

'Just one of my evening-class students needing some extra tuition.'

'Right.' He waited.

She was scarlet now, to the roots of her hair.

'His name? I need to know his name.'

She looked past him towards the corner of the room and said, quietly, 'David.'

He wrote that down and, once again, waited for a surname. When nothing came he looked up enquiringly, but her gaze was still on the corner and her mouth firmly closed.

'Oh,' he murmured, 'I see.' He put down his pen. 'David the gardener?'

'Yes,' she said. 'And no, you don't see.'

While Carol looked up Singlewood Nursery in *Yellow Pages*, Bridgeman and Jenny went upstairs to view the jewellery. If he thought it looked promising he wasn't saying.

Jenny put his new coolness down to him being busy and distracted, but she suspected it otherwise. Well, what was it to do with him? Even if she was carrying on with David. Which begged another question, where *was* David?

'Your friend didn't turn up, after all,' said Bridgeman when they were back in the kitchen.

'Obviously not.'

He didn't have to make it sound as if she had been stood up.

'Pity. Might have saved us some work.'

She glanced around at the crowded kitchen, stiff with police both uniform and plain clothes, and white-overalled SOCOs and forensic staff, all busy phoning, writing, using lap tops and depositing their equipment. 'Maybe he realized that this was not a good time.'

He shrugged. 'Maybe he was frightened off.'

That was ridiculous, thought Jenny, but said nothing.

Carol looked up from her *Yellow Pages*. 'Nothing in here.'

Bridgeman grimaced, sighed heavily and said to Jenny, 'Well, you can regain Brownie points by giving DC Smith here as detailed a description as possible of your gardener student. With your artistic eye it should be particularly acute.'

What a cheek! thought Jenny. Regain Brownie points, indeed! Who did the man think he was? No wonder his wife had left him. Carol merely glanced at her sergeant in surprise. Obviously, this was not his usual style. Did he think she knew more than she was saying, and want to unsettle her? Was that his game?

'I can do better than describe him,' she said crisply, 'I can draw him for you.'

145

'That would be extremely helpful,' Bridgeman said stiffly. 'And while you're at it, you might manage to perform a similar service with regard to Mr Furness.'

'I don't think I could do that.'

'Why not?'

'I only saw him the once. And then when I . . . when I was concentrating on other things.' She stopped and felt herself colouring up again.

'What?'

'I meant to tell you when it happened, but I felt I must have been mistaken.'

'When *what* happened?'

'I thought I saw him in London.'

Bridgeman stood quite still and gazed at her in wonderment. 'You *what*?'

'I was going to see an art dealer and I was on the bus in Bond Street and I looked out of the window . . .' – she knew she was babbling but couldn't stop herself – 'and I saw this man out of the window. . . .'

The telephone rang and Bridgeman nodded Carol to answer it. 'I've got to hear the end of this,' he murmured.

'And I thought he looked familiar, but I couldn't think where I had seen him. Then it dawned on me he looked like Mr Furness and I turned around to get another look, but he was gone. He must have turned the corner into Grafton Street and. . . .' Carol was hovering. She put her hand up and waved to attract Bridgeman's eye.

'What *is* it?' he snapped.

'Hope you're ready for this,' she murmured, ignoring his bad temper.

'I think,' he said, 'I'm starting to be ready for absolutely anything.'

'Not this, you're not,' said Carol, shaking her head in disbelief. 'The body,' she grimaced ruefully, 'not only is it middle-aged,' she paused again before delivering the *coup de grâce*, 'but it's male.'

146

17

'These are our priorities,' Glass announced at the early morning briefing. He looked as immaculate and on the ball as ever but every now and then he removed his rimless spectacles to rub under his tired eyes. He pointed to the blackboard. 'Priority one: identifying the body. Priority two: tracing Furness. The first is not going to be easy due to its condition. We did think they might be one and the same, but our witness says Furness is tall and slim with dark-brown hair and eyes while Mr Outhouse Two is five feet eight inches tall, of muscular build, with curly, faded, gingery hair. So that's that out of the window.

'So we have no idea who the victim is, not even whether he is local. His build and the scar suggest he might be sporty, so it could be worth looking at local rugby clubs and so on.

'Sergeant Bridgeman is still conducting a thorough search of the Furness property, looking for further info. Meanwhile, we'll organize a house-to-house, coupling questions about the victim and Mr Furness. The man can't have lived here without making some impact on the community. Someone must have supplied him with newspapers, garden plants, groceries, library books, money.

'We should get more from this gardener, David, whom we've located and is on his way in. He might also be a suspect so keep an ear open about him.

'The house-sitting agency has been of no help. They usually interview clients personally, but when they are busy that some-

147

times goes out the window which, sod's law, it did this time.' He looked up from his notes and around at the troops who were looking rather confused. Time for a rallying cry, thought Carol.

'I know this case has become ludicrously complex – if it is all one case, that is. The thing to do is not to try to keep it all in your head. Just concentrate on the tasks in hand while being alert for any other nuance, however slight. Don't let anything escape you – concerning schoolgirls, photography, Rolls, Jenny and Robin. . . .'

Oh, thanks, thought Carol. You made it better, then you made it worse. You *must* be tired.

Glass seemed to have sensed her reaction. 'Do your best chaps and chapesses,' he said, in a manner which, for him, was remarkably lightweight. 'I can't ask anything more.'

Despite having been told that the visit was not concerning news of Linda, Mrs Blackstone was shaking when she greeted Carol. Now, she looked hunted as she sat on their threadbare settee, one hand grasping the other so as to still the tremble.

'But, I only met Mr Furness once,' she insisted. 'I wouldn't know him again if I bumped into him in the street.'

'Don't worry,' said Carol cheerfully, 'we're just building up a picture from several sources. We're talking to lots of people.'

She seemed relieved at that. It was a lie. They had no idea yet whether they would be able to find any other people who knew Furness. For all they knew he might have lived out at Berry Hill House in complete isolation only having contact with tradesmen via the phone – and even banking elsewhere. But the woman was clearly coming apart and, if she did, they'd get nothing at all out of her. She had deteriorated markedly since Carol last saw her. Her eyes were even redder-rimmed and the mousy roots of her unwashed, dyed-black hair were more than half-an-inch in length now.

'Any idea how tall he might be?'

'Oh, I don't know – er, let me see – quite tall.'

'About six foot?'

'Oh, I don't think so, a bit less than that I'd say.' Her hands tightened on each other. 'But I might be wrong. I'm not much good with heights.'

'Not to worry.' Carol reached for the mug of tea Mrs Blackstone had insisted on providing and took a sip, before asking casually, 'His build? Fat? Thin? Muscly?

'Oh, oh just ordinary, I think.'

'Right. A bit on the slim side, perhaps?'

She shook her head, 'I don't think so. I mean he was wearing an anorak so it was difficult to tell.'

Carol tried to hide her disappointment murmuring, 'Fine', and jotted down the useless information. Watch for every nuance, Glass had said. He must be joking. Members of the public were so bad at descriptions. Some people couldn't even tell you the colour of their beloved's eyes. This was certainly not going to take them any further forward than the brief description that Jenny had given them.

'His colouring?'

Panic came into the woman's eyes. Bad phrase, Carol.

'Can you remember what colour his hair was?'

'Sort of fair, I think.'

'Right,' Carol groaned inwardly. This was worse than useless. One thing they already did know was that the man's hair was dark and if she got that wrong there was little point in going on. She looked at her watch, 'Oh dear,' she exclaimed. 'Oh dear, I've got to go. I've got an appointment.' Which was true, she was going to the kennels to interview the staff she'd missed yesterday, but it wasn't really pressing. 'Look, I'll talk to you again later, if that's OK?'

'Sorry if I've not been much help. I don't feel very well.'

'Oh, nonsense, you've been very helpful. I thought you looked a bit poorly.'

'Flu, I think.'

'Well, you get yourself tucked up in bed.' She closed her note-book. 'Do you need anything, some shopping?'

'No, that's all right. My neighbour will help me. I just feel awful that I haven't been able to help.'

'Nonsense. You've done fine. Takes time for things to come back into your mind and, as you said, you only saw him once and that was a long time ago. Have a little think later and if anything occurs to you, just jot it down. I'll be back to see you.'

Sailing prints adorned the spanking clean, parchment-coloured walls and on a nearby shelf perched a shrunken head and a tomahawk.

'Travelled a lot,' confided Andy Fairsmith, the secretary of the Birchfield and Louden Rugby club. 'That's Navajo.' He picked up the tomahawk. 'Genuine article, too.'

They were talking in the sitting-room. Outside, was a tranquil but excessively neat flower garden. Any fallen leaf or wilting bloom would get short shrift there, thought Doggie.

He had expected a younger man than Andy. Nonetheless, the man did have the look of a prop forward – big all over. About six foot two in height and shoulders with which you wouldn't quarrel. The face was golden-pink, freckled, and wore an open, guileless expression. His shock of fair hair was greying a little at the temples and there were no signs of rugby's rumbustious, beer-swilling, reputation. The aura was more one of honesty, decency, rectitude and concerned citizenship which, as Doggie was aware, might not mean a blind thing.

'This secretary thing is partly my way of keeping in the rugby scene,' Andy confided with a self-deprecating grin. 'I still play a bit. One or two of us oldies still struggle on, reluctant to let go. We get chiacked by the youngsters but they know we have our uses. Occasionally our experience tells in the game itself, but mainly they tolerate us to keep up the numbers, train the young-sters and do the boring organizing bit.

Doggie confided that it was about such a couple of oldies that he was calling. It seemed that Mr Furness was not a man to pop into the local newsagents for a paper and a packet of cigarettes.

Neither did he bank in Birchfield or have a library ticket. So they were pursuing other avenues.

He began with the non-runner. Personally, he couldn't see the slim, well-spoken and apparently reclusive Mr Furness all muddied in the scrum. 'We just want to trace Mr Furness to eliminate him from our enquiry,' said Doggie, bending the truth a little.

'Furness? No.' He shook his head. 'The bloke out at Berry Hill House, you mean? I heard you had some trouble out there.'

Bad news travels fastest, thought Doggie. And they imagined they'd managed to keep a lid on it for a few hours.

'No,' said Andy, 'Furness isn't a member. You could try the cricket club. I would imagine that would be more his style.'

Suddenly, Doggie was all attention. 'You know him?'

'Oh, yes. He's in Rotary.'

This is not a good day, thought Carol. I might as well go home and get back into bed. The couple who helped run the animal refuge did remember Avril as one of the volunteer helpers. Also that she was 'a sweet kid' and loved animals. What else?

But, no, they couldn't recall any particular relationships with other volunteers. It was understandable. Theirs was a busy life – judging from the number of interruptions during Carol's questioning: admissions and their inevitable paperwork, examinations and decisions; constant calls about lost pets, found pets, pets wanted; and members of the public popping in and out to view.

'Sorry about this,' said the woman, jumping up yet again to attend an enquirer, 'but we have to keep open house or we'd never re-home any.'

Carol tried to contain her irritation. She had imagined that someone else would take charge while she interviewed the couple. But at least they had come up with the list of volunteers she had requested, such as it was. Some had first names only with brief descriptions, 'Gerry – teenage lad, tall, dark hair, wears glasses', but a few full names and addresses were included. They should keep her busy for a while and meanwhile they might be able to fill in some other names.

Before leaving, Carol strolled through to the animal compound. She just had to see whether the tiny, one-eyed, yelping Yorkie was still there, shivering in the huge, concrete kennel. She half thought she might rescue it for the girls while telling herself she was half out of her mind. Who would look after it during the day when she was at work and the girls at school? Perhaps, for a consideration, she could persuade their ever-obliging neighbour, Mrs Holding. But wasn't that asking a bit too much? It could all go horribly wrong. The dog might be mentally disturbed, attack the Holdings' cat, yelp all day, not be house-trained. Wouldn't it be more sensible just to let things be?

She was both disappointed and relieved when she reached the kennel to find it empty.

'Has the Yorkie been homed?' she asked the young lad who was swilling out the floor.

'Nah,' he replied, 'it's having its picture took, innit.'

Carol was jubilant as she hurried towards the small field where the photo shoot was taking place.

'That's it! That's it!' she exclaimed, as what had been lurking at the back of her mind suddenly popped straight to the front. Who took those photographs displayed on the outside of the kennels and cages? Could it be someone who used double catch-lights when taking portraits of young girls?

18

Furness had done an excellent job of wiping the house clean of his personality, reflected Bridgeman. Forensics might come up with something, particularly with regard to the locked room and the outhouse, but that would scarcely help in building a personal picture of the man. As Jenny had noticed, there were no photographs on display but, more oddly, there weren't any in cupboards or drawers either. Neither was there any personal correspondence, only that concerning the household utilities like electricity and gas. The impression was that the man had not intended to return. If so, why had he bothered to phone? To find out whether anyone had found the body?

Bridgeman left the house virtually empty-handed – apart from the green folder he'd discovered half-hidden among utilities files. Furness must have missed that one during his clearance. Not that it held any personal correspondence – merely stuff relating to his membership of clubs and societies. But that was something, wasn't it? He took the folder to peruse at his leisure, or at least, during lulls in managing the incident-room. Things were fairly quiet there, now that most of the troops had gone out on door-to-door enquiries and Glass was interviewing David, the gardener.

It was early in the afternoon when he removed the contents and began to go through them systematically, a notebook by his right hand. He turned the pile over and started from the bottom. First out proved to be a mish-mash of the Birchfield Players old play programmes, membership cards and correspondence. Clearly their repertoire had been lightweight stuff. The green and white programme for *Blithe Spirit* – listed Furness as the husband while Mrs Furness took the role of the madcap ghost, Madame Arcati. Oh well, the pair had clearly had something in common then.

Cuttings from the *Birchfield and Louden Messenger* spoke of the club's 'enthusiastic' performances which was a bit of a giveaway. In one clipping their long-suffering reviewer congratulated Mr Furness on his lifelike, crude and rude Squire Fortescue in *Now is the Time*, a rustic comedy by one Harvey Blincote. This scarcely tallied with Jenny's description of a suave, sophisticate – clearly the man was a consummate performer despite the drawbacks of his amdram society. The study of all those luvvy books on his shelves had obviously paid off.

It was a bizarre sight – the seedy Jake Runsmith on his knees zooming in on the tiny, lopsided face of Dinky, the one-eyed Yorkie.

Sensing her presence, he looked up and muttered laconically, 'You get around.'

'You, too.'

He stood up. 'OK,' he said to the boyish young woman hovering out of camera shot, 'got any more?'

'Just the one, a GSD called Minx.'

'Wheel her on.'

Carol took the Yorkie from the young woman while she went off to get the German Shepherd, 'I didn't have you down as a dog lover,' she said.

'I'm not. It's just a job. The weekly rag does this piece on adorable animals wanting perfect homes.'

The Yorkie was in ecstasies at so much attention, its trembling body writhing and wriggling as it struggled to lick Carol's face.

'Yes, I've seen it.' In fact, that's where Jackie had got the idea, she recalled. 'Remind me – how often does it come out, this heart-wrenching feature?'

'Once a month – with an extra after Christmas when people are busy dumping their adorable pet prezzies.'

Cynical bugger. You really are an extremely unattractive little man, thought Carol. He was almost runtish, she noticed, with his skinny frame, long nose and prominent Adam's apple. His 'uniform' seemed to accentuate his worst points. The skin-tight black T-shirt and grubby black jeans clinging to his angular body and the facial studs and ear-rings drawing attention to his unhealthy grey complexion and greasy hair. The whole effect was of small-time circus roustabout-cum-new age traveller.

'Now you want to know whether it's always me that takes the pics?' Jake said, giving her a sharp look.

She shrugged nonchalantly, 'Something like that. But nothing sinister. I just want to have a word with all the people who turn up here regularly – in case they remember Avril.'

'The girl who was done in?'

'As you so nicely put it, yes.'

'An' she was one of the volunteers here?'

'Correct.'

He gave her an old-fashioned look. They both knew it wasn't as simple as that. She not only wanted to know if Jake had made contact, but if that contact had led elsewhere. To photo sessions, for example? He might be physically repellent to Carol, but his impressively high-tech camera with its long lens gave him a certain authority and, very probably, otherwise unattainable access to nubile young women. In particular, those desperate to be models.

The GSD began straining at the leash and barking frenziedly. She was excited by the presence of Dinkie who was now giving Carol a good wash down. Jake gave Carol a sour look so, reluctantly, she handed the little one-eyed Yorkie back to the sturdy young volunteer. As she took it away it yelped pitifully and struggled madly towards her. Carol forced her attention back to Jake and the fact that he had not yet answered her question.

Dinkie gone, Minx settled down to the business of transforming herself into the most beautiful dog in the world with that soppy, aren't-I-gorgeous? expression some canines can summon up to order.

As a result they quickly had 'a wrap' as Jake put it and while they strolled back to the office he began to talk.

'I do *some* of the local rag's shoots – when the staff man is busy or can't be bothered. Could have met this Avril in the same way that I just "met" that girl bringing in the pooches. But, like you saw, it was no blinking social occasion. I didn't even get to know that girl's name and if I did meet Avril here I wouldn't have known hers either. I don't remember her face, that's for sure. I'm just in, do the business, then out again. No hanging about.'

It was quite a long speech for him and all freely volunteered. In fact, Carol now realized, it was he who had posed the question in the first place. Odd? Or just native cunning? Getting in first? And Carol did see what he meant. But she also saw that today's assistant had hardly been comely. That, she suspected, could make all the difference. Also, the fact that a policewoman was looking on might well have cramped Runsmith's usual style.

Furness was a member of the local Rotary, Bridgeman noted, as he continued his trudge through the green folder. He also subscribed to a club known only by its initials: The NNFYD Club. A large compliment slip was the only witness to the latter's existence. On it, scrawled in black ink, 'Catalogue enclosed. I think you'll agree, more endless delight!' There was also some correspondence, relating to 'the session' Furness was arranging for a man called Belton but no mention of what the 'session' entailed.

There was a much-thumbed, *Speakers for Rotary Clubs* list and a couple of Rotary dinner menus, one of them emblazoned with assorted signatures. That could be useful.

'Ah, this is more like it,' Bridgeman muttered to himself as he came upon a batch of newspaper cuttings. He felt a tingle of anticipation.

One group photograph captioned, 'Members talking to round-the-world yachtsman, Fergus O'Keen', listed those present from left to right and Furness was one of them. Bridgeman's eyes raced to and fro from the caption to the photograph. Damn. The figure marked down as Furness was turned away. Damn it – he was looking towards their esteemed guest who must have been extremely tall, judging by how he towered over Furness, who, according to Jenny, was himself no dwarf. Indeed, his back view looked much stockier than Bridgeman had imagined.

Never mind, plough on. Can't be lucky every time. Another photograph, under the headline, *Men's Health in the Spotlight*, was a handing-over shot in which, usually, both parties face front, looking at the camera rather than each other. The caption read 'Rotarian, Isaac Furness, presents Dr Alwyn Peters with a cheque for £2,000'. Bridgeman couldn't believe it, Furness was turned away *again* facing the doctor – another tall man. Was it deliberate? Did Furness not want his image recorded? If so, why not keep a lower profile? At least in this photograph he could see part of Furness's side view which was craggier than he had expected. Never mind. Plough on.

Eureka! A photograph in which everyone, but everyone, was facing forward. He skipped through the caption.

'HAND OVER: Birchfield Rotary's new secretary, Alan J. Bird, accepts powers of office from retiring secretary George Blenkinsop. Left to Right:. . . .'

Bridgeman's eyes raced along the line of names until he came to Furness. He looked up to the person indicated and frowned in puzzlement. Couldn't be. He counted along the row, yes – fourth from the left. Good grief! He didn't believe it! Slipping from underneath the newspaper's black-and-white version was a full colour print of the same photograph. He gazed at it, stunned. Sandy hair, stocky build, blue eyes. . . .

So engrossed was Bridgeman that he wasn't aware that

Doggie Edwards had entered the room and was now hovering over him.

Edwards cleared his throat and said, 'I've got news for you.' Bridgeman looked up. 'That Furness. . . .'

'I know,' said Bridgeman. 'He's the victim. It was *his* body in the outhouse.'

19

The noise in the murder room reached a crescendo as those who had already heard the latest news passed it on to new arrivals, relishing their gobsmacked expressions. The hubbub died instantly Glass marched in, looking on form and sleekness itself in his impeccable, dark-navy suit, blue-grey shirt and light-navy tie shot through with faintest of silver-blue glints.

He glanced over at Bridgeman's new 'connections' map which had the appearance of a ragged family tree. Solid lines linked up all the players who had a known connection – Avril with Linda and Linda with Furness and so on – while dots joined the likes of Avril and Runsmith where the connections were less sure.

'Looks good,' Glass nodded. 'Right, listen up, chaps. As you have all doubtless heard by now, this case has become even more complicated, if that's possible. The body found in the Berry Hill House outbuilding, which we confidently expected to be female, turned out to be male, which suggested that the house-owner, Furness, might be a prime suspect. Now, we find that the body is that of Furness.

'So, why was he murdered? We have no evidence that he was a homosexual or involved in anything criminal – often the case in this type of mysterious male murder. He has no criminal record which, of course, is not to say that he wasn't involved in something murky. So, the possibility of it being a contract job is still on the cards but, if so, it's a mighty strange one.

159

'A personal vendetta? Was he carrying on with someone's wife? His own wife had left him and is reported as saying that he was a man who strayed. It's urgent that we find her, of course. Smith and Edwards have already made a start checking data bases, utility companies etc. Any bright ideas welcome. She's a rather curious figure in all this – suddenly putting in an appearance a couple of days ago. Was she involved in the murder and sent to spy out the land by our mystery man? Up to something on her own? We need to know more about her. Back to Furness. Was he involved in paedophilia or a porn ring of some kind? Perhaps things had gone too far, he was getting jittery and wanted out – so had to be disposed of? Was this where Linda and Avril fitted in?' He pointed to Bridgeman's map. 'There's a definite connection with Avril and the Furnesses.

'Obviously, the key to all this is the man who handed over Berry Hill House to the house-sitters. Who is he? The agency has been no help. It's their policy to visit potential clients where possible, but sometimes, due to lack of time, are obliged to accept bookings over the phone and leave it to the house-sitter's judgement whether the premises are acceptable when they go to see them. Which is what happened in this case. Therefore, they did not know that the man they spoke to was *not* Furness, the owner. There is no obligation for the client to say where they are going – only to give a contact for emergencies – and this one has turned out to be bogus. No such person exists. We are busy checking with British Telecom regarding the phonecall from Australia but it's my feeling that, too, will turn out to be bogus, particularly since the house-sitter thought she spotted him in London, which is probably where he was calling from.

'But why did our man, our prime suspect, keep in touch from Australia or wherever? Just to find out whether the body had been discovered? He could have read about that in his newspaper. So, is there something else on his mind? Something still on the premises he wants or is likely to point to him? Don't ask me!' he exclaimed suddenly, shaking his head. 'Buggered if I know!' Everyone burst out laughing and relaxed a little.

160

He waited until the mirth had subsided.

'All we have to go on with this Furness substitute is a scant description and a tentative photofit culled from the house-sitter, Jenny Warrender, which you all have in front of you. The gardener, David Spinks, is no help. He claims only to have met the real Mr Furness and to have no knowledge of the contents of the outhouse or any other strange goings-on at the premises. But then he would say that, wouldn't he? We'll be working on him some more but he's been co-operative and we've taken DNA samples.

'Which brings me to another matter. This young woman, Miss Warrender, seems to be the only person who can identify our mystery man so she might be in some danger. You, Carol, and DC Staines will alternate guarding her when her boyfriend is not there, and you'll also act as family liaison officers.' Great, thought Carol. Thanks a bunch. Got no babies for me to look after?

In some ways Jenny felt a sense of relief. She *hadn't* just been imagining things after all. There *had* been something very wrong with the house. Robin couldn't pooh-pooh that! Every now and then she relived the terrible moment 'it' had fallen on top of her. Then the horror and terror rose in her throat again and she felt so panic-stricken she wanted to scream and scream.

Oddly, she didn't feel so frightened of the house now. Not that she had been alone in it since. Quite the opposite. SOCOs still lingered, poking about, dabbing at things, taking impressions and 'bagging', as they called it and, of course, Robin was there. An abjectly apologetic Robin, still not quite recovered from the shock of arriving back home late last night to be greeted by the sight of swarming police and ghostly flocks of men and women in white paper suits. He was fussing about, waiting on Carol and Jenny with tea and biscuits. Oddly, though he knew about it, he had not yet commented on her appointment with David. Wasn't he curious? He must be, surely? As for the police suspicion of David, that was ridiculous. He was only a gardener, for heaven's sake. Of *course* he didn't know what was in the outhouse. She'd never seen him go near the place. Carol assured her that their interest was merely routine but the police always said that, didn't they?

It came as a bit of a shock when Carol told her that whenever Robin was going to leave the house they would have to inform her so that she, or another detective, could replace him.

'Whatever for?'

At first Carol didn't answer, then she said gently, 'We think you might need protection and – since you refuse to leave.'

'We can't leave. We've nowhere else to go – except our little caravan!'

Carol grimaced. 'That would be worse. I think. Look, there must be somewhere else. Relatives? Friends?'

There were. But Jenny hated staying with other people and the constraints that imposed on her – particularly when she was trying to work. Besides, there was so much to paint here. And what if she went away and David called? She needed to see him, to warn him he was under suspicion, just because of their innocent appointment. He might not come if he realized she was not alone.

'We could find you somewhere,' Carol suggested.

Jenny shook her head. 'No.'

'Well then, I'm sorry, but one of us will have to be here when Robin goes out. You are the only person who has seen the man we all thought was Furness. There's no point in putting your life at risk for the sake of a bit of privacy. It will only be temporary and nobody is going to interfere with your work. I'll be too busy keeping a lookout for strangers – and studying for my sergeant's exam – to bother you, believe me.'

Jenny was suitably chastened. They were only trying to look after her and it was a change for somebody to want to do that.

'Sorry. OK. That's fine.' She paused, 'I suppose it's just that that bossy Sergeant Bridgeman has put my back up with the police interference.'

Carol glared at her. 'You should be grateful that Sergeant

Bridgeman took enough interest to want to pop in to see you last night!'

Jenny was now mortified. 'Oh, God! Of course, of course. I didn't mean it really. I'm just confused and – well – he and I don't always seem to hit if off.'

'He's a good man,' insisted Carol, gripping the edges of her briefcase very hard, 'who has been having a bad time.'

'Oh, yes. His wife left him, he said.'

'Well, maybe what he *didn't* tell you was that it was because he got so involved in trying to catch a sickening rapist that she scarcely saw him. Then, when he had the man pinned down, he saw him get away with it through the lies put across by a cynical lawyer. Who, by the way, also did his best to ruin Sergeant Bridgeman's reputation.'

There was a palpable silence. Jenny did not know what to say and, at the same time, sensed that Carol felt she may have said too much. She certainly seemed to care about her superior. Police loyalty, Jenny supposed. Carol locked her briefcase and stood up. 'I'll have a word with Robin before I go,' she said.

There was no doubt that Robin was an attractive man. Carol could see that although, for her, he was a bit too charming. However, unlike Jenny, he was certainly going out of his way to be co-operative and pleasant.

'I'm so grateful for what you did. That you were there when she needed you,' he assured her, his dark eyes losing their knowing look and becoming warmly sincere. 'Whatever you think is best now, I'll happily go along with,' he insisted.

'Well, the most important thing is, we must be given notice whenever you're obliged to leave Jenny alone in the house,' said Carol.

'I won't,' he said firmly. 'Not from now on. Not until this is all over. I've learned my lesson.' Suddenly, he looked vulnerable and rather young. 'I was in such a panic when I thought I'd lost her, I can't tell you.' He seemed near to tears and Carol began to realize that the confident charm might be a bit of a façade. He grimaced ruefully. 'I think I've been a bit selfish. Bad timer and all that,' he finished, managing a grin, reverting to his jaunty self.

'Well, if something comes up and you have to leave her alone, just let us know,' Carol insisted. 'Meanwhile, we'll fit a couple of panic buttons, one upstairs and one down. Don't hesitate to use them if you have any doubts about your security. We'll respond to them instantly. And we'll see to it that patrol cars pay regular attention to the place. To tell the truth, we wanted to put a permanent guard here, but. . . .' She spread her hands.

'Manpower, I know.'

'We're at full stretch with this wretched business.'

Her mobile rang. 'Get back here, pronto,' said Bridgeman. 'We've got a good suspect in.'

'Great!' Could it be all over? She crossed her fingers. She might be able to give Bella that birthday party after all. 'Who is it?'

'Nobody you'd know,' he said. 'A lorry driver by the name of Eddie Bates.'

20

The bulky, green-overalled figure of Eddie Bates stood, trembling, in front of the interview-room table. He certainly has the build to subdue any young girl, thought Bridgeman, and who were more gifted with opportunity for rape and murder than long-distance lorry drivers?

True, they did tend to commit their crimes well away from home – which would not be the case if Eddie Bates had abducted and murdered Avril Scanscombe. Eddie was a local man who lived in one of the run-down farm cottages on the edge of Hedgecote, a hamlet scarcely three miles outside Birchfield. Could be that a sudden opportunity arose close to home and he'd taken it without thinking too hard about the consequences?

'Mr Bates, *please*, sit down,' he said. 'We can't get this sorted out if you won't sit down.' And, he thought to himself, you'll have to do some nifty talking to get out of this. The evidence against Bates was coming from so many different sources that the accumulated pile looked substantial.

The big man just stood there, wringing his hands together in a childlike way, and looking pleadingly at Bridgeman.

'If you've done nothing wrong, you have nothing to fear,' Bridgeman insisted. Inwardly, he cursed those television programmes which peddled the idea that practically everyone who had ever been arrested for a serious crime was innocent, but had had a confession wrung out of them, nonetheless.

165

Personally, he couldn't recall anyone confessing to anything of which he wasn't damn sure they were guilty.

'Come on, man,' he said, patting the chair firmly. 'We're busy people. I've offered you a solicitor and I can't do more than that.'

Suddenly, Eddie grasped at his green woolly hat, dragging it off over his forehead leaving his short, toffee-coloured hair sticking out at all angles. He looked like a bedraggled teddy bear. At last, he sat down, saying quite belligerently, 'I ain't done nothing.'

He certainly didn't look like a vicious murderer. But then, who did? As for their own protestations of innocence, it seemed to Bridgeman that even those caught up to their elbows in their victim's blood were able to persuade themselves that they were innocent – or at the very least, someone else was to blame. Usually the victim.

Was the man subnormal, Bridgeman had wondered when he was brought in? If so, he'd better cover himself by getting some professional help before interviewing him. However, the DS had soon realized that Bates was merely a man of limited intelligence and experience. The latter, possibly due to shyness or social inadequacy which, in turn, fitted him snugly into the prime suspect category. A shy, inadequate loner. Classic stuff.

'First of all,' Bridgeman asked, after he had informed the lorry driver of his rights, 'did you know Avril Scanscombe?'

He knew damn well he did.

''Course,' Bates nodded. He glanced from Bridgeman to Carol and back again. 'But I wouldn't *do* nothing to her!'

'We didn't say you did,' said Bridgeman. 'Look, just relax and tell us the truth.'

So, he had admitted knowing the girl. Well, he'd been seen by witnesses, so why not admit it? Smart move.

'She was ever such a nice girl,' Bates insisted suddenly. 'It was terrible what happened. Terrible. I couldn't believe it, you know.' He shook his big head from side to side in disbelief, his face looking pathetically and genuinely bereft.

'Tell us how you got to know her.'

'Used to give her lifts, didn't I?'

They waited for him to continue.

'She was ever so good,' he said in a rush. 'She always played with my Markie. The other girls wouldn't.'

Bridgeman and Carol remained motionless, not allowing a flicker of interest to creep into their expressions.

'Your Markie?' Bridgeman asked eventually, his voice quiet and casual. 'Er, what exactly is that, Eddie?'

Eddie stared at them as though they were daft. 'My dog, 'course.' He gave a lopsided half smile. 'He's a boxer, an' the other girls say he's too slobbery – but Avril never did.' They waited again. He seemed uncertain what they wanted next so he went back to where he had left off. 'Always comes out with me. Keeps me company.' He looked from one to the other, then offered, 'He's a good guard dog, as well.'

Jenny couldn't believe it. Everything was back to how it once had been with Robin. They talked, laughed together, and made wild, passionate love. More, he seemed to *want* to be there, with her, not up in town with his cronies. He took the trouble to ask her about her work, her opinions, and made her laugh with his quirky humour – just as he used to do when they started out. Maybe, at last, he was growing out of that world of constant adolescence and entering the real world with her.

He was also prepared to discuss alternate ways of making a living. At first, they did involve using his advertising expertise in freelance consulting but, more and more, he responded to her plea that they look around and see how they could capitalize on what they already had. For example, when they were house-sitting, why not offer to do painting and decorating as well? What nicer for a client than to return from a holiday and find that neglected room all freshly painted and papered?

'Right,' he enthused. 'All the gain and no pain.'

'And,' said Jenny excitedly, 'I could offer to bake batches of my biscuits, and tarts, for their freezers!'

'Which they could pass off as their own at dinner parties!'

167

The beauty of these schemes was that they wouldn't require financial investment. Unlike his plans for making more money from her paintings – a new and surprising enthusiasm. He had even 'taken on board' the idea of the village-hall show and was all fired up about printing her efforts as greetings cards – and calendars as well. She didn't want to dampen his new and welcome eagerness, but she couldn't see where they would get the money to back this little scheme. 'Another possibility, in the same vein,' she said lightly, 'would be to tout my paintings around the greetings card makers.'

'They'd rip you off.'

'No, not necessarily.' She shook her head. 'Anyway, I keep the copyright.'

'Huh. I bet we could make much more doing it on our own.'

'Maybe, but they've got the outlets. Going out and selling them ourselves would not be easy and would take a lot of time.' She patted his hand. 'Why don't we take a good look at the options first.'

'Right,' he said, rubbing his hands and grinning. 'Meanwhile, Mrs Picasso, get painting.'

'What we would like to know,' Bridgeman asked, leaning forward encouragingly, 'is how you got to know Avril.'

'At the kennels.'

'Oh, you go there, do you?'

'Yeah. I did. That's where I got Markie,' he explained. 'He'd been treated terrible, see, and when he got better they let me adopt him.'

'Oh, isn't that nice,' said Carol. 'I'm thinking of taking one of their dogs.'

'You won't be sorry, miss,' Bates assured her earnestly. 'Markie's a real pal to me.'

'So you met Avril there, then you saw her again later?' persisted Bridgeman.

He nodded, 'Yeah, a couple of times. First off I went back so they could tell me how to look after Markie. An' there was this other dog, Bounce, I used to take along when I took Markie out before they gave him to me. So I went back to see how Bounce was getting on and give him a walk. He and Markie were friends, d'you see?'

'I do,' Bridgeman assured him. 'So when was it you gave Avril lifts?' he persisted.

'If she was leaving the same time as me or if I saw her on the road coming back from the kennels. I used to pass that way – on one of my routes.'

'Was that often?'

He thought about that, then slowly shook his head. 'Not really. She'd go up on Fridays, I knew that, so I'd look out for her. But she didn't *always* come. Then, 'course' – he looked sad – 'she went away altogether.'

'And that upset you?'

He looked surprised at that remark. 'Well, 'course. She was my friend, wasn't she?'

'What we can't understand,' said Bridgeman rather more sharply, 'is why you didn't come forward earlier?'

He looked disconcerted, mumbled something then looked away.

'I didn't catch that,' said Bridgeman.

Bates took a deep breath and said, 'I'd lose my job.'

'For giving Avril a lift?'

'Giving any girl a lift. It's not allowed. Boss don't want no trouble.'

'But when we were trying to identify the body you must have realized how important that was? When you saw the picture of your friend in the paper.'

'Oh, I didn't think *that* was her! Didn't look like her and, anyway, she'd gone away, see?'

Robin had his head down, deep among printers' brochures and sample cards, looking as happy as a sandboy. Jenny had to admit a sense of excitement, too, at the idea of one of her paintings gracing a greetings card.

169

Robin had mooted another idea on his return from the library carrying an armload of art instruction books.

'You could do one of these, piece of cake,' he said. 'I could do the writing.'

'But, darling, I'm not a professional. I'm self-taught and only good at painting certain things.'

'Bet these lot are, too. It's all a racket. Look at them. Seems to me all you need is a gimmick. Some formula that pretends it's easy.' He spread the books on the kitchen-table with an expansive flourish, 'See?'

He pointed to the titles: *Two-stroke painting*, *Who Says You Can't Paint!* and *Painting Can Be Easy and It's Fun!* 'Then you start selling your own, must-have, patent brushes and other paraphernalia – and look what they charge for instruction videos? Gold mine. Piece of cake.'

Jenny was beginning to understand why Robin got into trouble at work. He had plenty of flair, but his feet were not planted firmly enough. On the other hand, were hers too solidly planted? She knew she shared some of his feelings about the books and videos which offered so much, but often delivered so little. Maybe, this *was* the time to take a chance?

So far, Eddie Bates's replies had been plausible. The reason he hadn't come forward to say he had seen Avril because he would get into trouble for giving lifts. As for not recognizing the picture – Bridgeman felt that didn't ring quite true. He thought the E-fit *did* look reasonably like the girl he later saw in photographs. Then again, Eddie seemed a simple soul and the lack of animation could have thrown him. He took a deep breath, but, he said to himself, let's see you get out of this, Mr Bates. He pursed his lips, then announced gravely, 'Mr Bates. On the path, the *only* path leading to Avril's body, was a size fourteen bootprint. A large size, you will agree?'

'Oh yeah, yeah.' He nodded. 'I take—'

Bridgeman stopped him with his hand. 'Would it surprise you

to know that those boots we took from you match the print exactly?'

Eddie was now shaking his head vehemently. He tried to speak but Bridgeman pressed on.

'Would it also surprise you to know that the tread of the wheelbarrow found in the back of your truck matches up perfectly with the wheelbarrow tread found near the scene?'

Bates got to speak at last. It came out explosively, in a jumble. 'No, yes. I mean – I was there. I was there.'

Bridgeman held his breath, then asked quietly, 'And *why* were you there, Mr Bates?'

'I was picking bluebells.'

'You were what?'

'Picking bluebells. It's Miss Warrender's watercolour class on Thursday evenings and I like painting flowers, and so does she. So I thought I would take her some, but bluebells don't last long so I picked them that afternoon.'

Bridgeman and Carol gazed at the huge man in disbelief. Eventually, Bridgeman found his voice. 'You need a *wheelbarrow* to pick bluebells?'

'Oh, yes. Well, you see it's so overgrown in there I had to really push through the bushes. I needed somewhere to put them so I could do that. And it's no good just having a few blue-bells – a lot looks much better so I needed the barrow to carry them.' He stopped, then looked from one stunned face to the other. 'Miss Warrender loves the flowers I get!' he exclaimed eagerly. 'Sometimes she gets the whole class to paint them!'

'That bloody woman!' exclaimed Bridgeman, standing up and throwing down his notes. 'Everything keeps coming back to that bloody woman!'

21

There was a chill about the house. Bridgeman, peering into his barren fridge, felt it more because he was tired. He was also hungry.

'Why couldn't you have thought about that before?' he chastized himself. 'You could have got a takeaway on the way home.'

No domestic slob, he was usually quite good at keeping up his food stocks. But this time the two eggs were well outdated, the remnants of bacon dry and curly and as for the cheese. 'Enough penicillin for a battalion of wounded soldiers,' he muttered as he chucked it in the bin. The freezer offered only a pepperoni and salami pizza which he didn't think his stomach would welcome at the moment. He shivered.

'First thing you need to do, matey,' he said, 'is get some heat in this place.' A human being to welcome me home would have been nice, too, he thought, contemplating the bleak sitting-room. 'Might stop you talking to yourself so much. That way lies . . . you know.' He switched on the table lamps and side lights to make the place look cheerier.

The phone rang. Should he answer? No. Bloody no. He'd been on the go for fourteen hours. Someone else could deal. But what if it was something vital? He sighed. He'd kick himself if he wasn't there for the breakthrough. Breakthrough? Huh. Fat chance. Bluebells! That was supposed to be a breakthrough. Bloody bluebells, the man had said and Jenny Warrender had confirmed it! Oh, what the hell. He picked up the receiver and plonked himself down on the hall chair.

'Hello, Derek?' said a soft, tentative voice.

Hannah.

He was so surprised he couldn't think of anything to say. After a lull he said, 'Hannah. How are you?' How is she? After walking out like that! How bloody *is* she!

'Fine,' she responded brightly, 'just fine.' He couldn't imagine what she wanted. She'd taken all her personal belongings and they were parleying in a civilized manner, via blood-sucking solicitors, about the house and furniture.

'Well, no, I'm not all right really,' she admitted, sounding tearful. He had a hunger headache coming on. 'I – I, well, to tell the truth, I've been missing you.'

His mind went blank. He wasn't prepared for this.

'Are you still there, Derek?'

'Yes, yes,' he parried. 'I was just taken by surprise. I've just come in and. . . .' It was she who had bloody left!

'I know it's a bad time. You're in the middle of a tough case. I've been reading about it and I realized it must be hard for you.'

Blimey, what next? 'Right. I—'

She cleared her throat and interrupted. 'I've also realized I might not have been as patient as I could have been over your work and. . . .' The speech sounded rehearsed and he felt touched. They had loved each other so much, once.

'No, no, Hanny. You had good reason. I mean, it can't have been very nice for you. . . . ' He'd told her that when she left. He'd sworn that if she stayed, he would try hard to make it different. It humiliated him now to remember how he'd cried and begged her to stay. But she had insisted that it was too late. He'd wondered then if there was someone else.

'Look, you're obviously very tired,' she said. 'Why don't we just meet up for a chat? No obligations.'

'Yes. A chat. Good idea.'

Was it? He had so accepted that she wasn't coming back and had got through some of the worst of the anguish. But he was longing for some contact with a human being not obsessed with murder and rape and other nastiness. 'I'd like that. I'd really like that,' he said, suddenly eager.

'Tomorrow? Lunchtime?'

'Yes, that's fine but—'

'I know, you might have to cancel. Just let me know. That's all I ask. You've got my mobile number. The Goat, then, at one o'clock. OK?'

'Right.'

When he put the phone down he felt warmer. She'd sounded as though she was worried about him. 'Have you had something to eat?' she'd asked, before she rang off. He'd lied and said yes. Now, he felt ravenous. He'd send out for an Indian takeaway. That would be good. He could tackle that now.

At last, some results were trickling in. It was almost as though Hannah's call last night had set good things in motion.

First, the stones and metals in the jewellery Jenny had found in the drawer had been declared 'similar' to those of which Avril's green-stoned ring were made. Better, some partial prints had been found on a necklace which had sufficient flat surface to be helpful. They hadn't been identified yet, of course. The DNA result on the semen in Avril's body was also back. There were two different codes: one for that in the mouth and another for that in the vagina. What they needed now were suspects whose fingerprints and codes matched. That's all. Maybe Furness's body would provide some?

'You look spruce and lively today,' said Carol, giving him the once-over. 'Dressed to impress, I'd say. Got a date?'

He nodded and grinned. 'With Hannah.'

'No!'

'She rang last night.'

'Well, I'm blowed.' She smiled encouragingly. 'Great.' The smile did not reach her eyes and he was sorry about that. 'Good for you.'

'Nothing settled. Just testing the water.'

'Well, fingers crossed.'

He looked at his watch. They were meeting in twenty minutes. Everything in the office was going smoothly. The date was on schedule. The more he thought about it, the more excited he felt. It had been a lonely time.

Doggie Edwards glanced up from his phone. 'Jake Runsmith has come in downstairs, Sarge. He wants a word.'

Bridgeman began to get up, but Carol put up a staying hand and pointed to her watch. 'I've been dealing with him, so I'll see him. No problem.' She pushed her chair back and got up. 'You keep your date.'

Bridgeman was torn. He wanted to be there – keep hands on – and this, he knew, was a turn-up. When witnesses suddenly called in of their own free will, it could be that they had suddenly remembered something vital. More likely, their consciences had at last pricked them, however belatedly, or, as they saw the truth emerging, they feared they might be implicated so wanted to get their oar in first. At such a time, even the small trickle they intended to spill could turn into a torrent; a torrent which could blow the case wide open. Maybe he would just listen in to the start of the interview and then leave Carol to it?

'He'll be better with me on my own,' she insisted, as she saw his hesitation. 'He thinks I'm a pussy cat and we don't want to frighten him with tigers at this stage, do we?'

He looked at her doubtfully then made a decision. 'OK. OK,' he nodded reluctantly. 'I'll be at The Goat if you need me.'

She waved an acknowledgement and left the room. He stood up himself. Might as well make a good impression by being early for his date. His date! The phone rang and he picked it up without thinking then grimaced and beckoned Doggie, miming him to be ready to take over.

'Sergeant Bridgeman? Hi, it's DI Weathers, Yard Porn Squad,' said a London voice. 'Look, mate, I've just been trawling the dirty pictures on the Internet.'

'Yes?' Bridgeman was puzzled.

'And I came across some dollies who I think might interest you.'

Doggie was hovering but Bridgeman put up his finger and mouthed, 'Just a minute'.

'Oh?'

'Yeh. Look, don't get your hopes up, mate, but I think one of them might be one of your missing girls, Linda Blackstone.'

'Bloody hell.'

The sight of Jake Runsmith was disconcerting. Not only was his demeanour less cocky than usual, but he actually stood up as Carol entered the room. That wasn't all. He had smartened himself up. Under his black leather jacket he was wearing a clean white shirt and pressed blue jeans. His right earlobe sported only one small, discreet, silver ear-ring and he had removed his nose ring.

Startled, Carol gestured for him to sit, then took the seat opposite and waited.

'Been thinking about these missing girls,' he began without preamble, 'and I realized that I might be able to help you after all.'

'We'd be grateful for any assistance,' she parroted ingratiatingly, pretending, like him, that he was not the truculent, unhelpful man she had previously encountered. This, she instantly recognized, was a vital moment. Being convincingly warm and friendly to repulsive, self-serving people was as important a detective skill as asking pertinent questions, and far more useful than the browbeating tactics beloved of TV and films. She kept very still, as though a quick movement on her part might scare him off, like a nervous bird.

'I suddenly remembered,' he confided, 'that I *did* take some pictures of one of those girls.'

'Really?' exclaimed Carol, looking surprised but not shocked.

'Yeh. That Cynthia. Nothing dirty, mind you.'

'Right.'

He stopped, adjusted his jacket and tugged at the unaccustomed shirt collar. 'Portraits at first. But, after a bit, we did do some topless. I'll cough to that. But that's nothing these days, is it?'

Carol shook her head. 'Hardly. So, where did you do this – photography?'

'Berry Hill House.'

'Right.' Carol nodded slowly. 'So, Mr Furness arranged it?'

'Yeh,' he agreed. 'An' the other bloke, of course.'

'The other bloke?' Carol forced her expression to remain bland, unmoved.

'Jones.'

She nodded casually. 'You got a bit more on him than that, Jake?' she asked her new friend. 'Like his first name, for instance?' She'd remain sugar sweet until he stopped giving, then, if she thought he was still holding anything back, she would threaten to charge him with every offence known to man.

'Oh, yeh. It was Bud, I think.' He paused and thought. 'Yeh, that was what Furness called him, Bud. 'Course, I don't know if that was his real monicker, do I? Sounds a bit iffy, don't it, Bud Jones? Usual thing in that business, false names.'

Carol was not about to go into the question of pseudonyms used in the porn business. She had a more important one to ask. 'You don't happen,' she said, as nonchalantly as her thumping heart would allow, 'to know where we might find this Bud Jones, do you, Jake?'

He shook his head firmly and shrugged. 'London, somewhere.'

'Any idea whereabouts?' she enquired lightly.

'Nah.'

Her euphoria began to evaporate. London. Bloody hell. Fifteen million, wasn't it?

Then a slow grin began to twitch across his unsavoury lips. 'But I have got his phone number – if you want it.'

Carol was torn between a desire to beat the man to death and overwhelming excitement which caused her to almost choke on her own breath.

Jake took his time reaching into his jacket pocket and pulling out a gold-embossed, red-leather diary. 'Had to contact him. He wanted me to do some of the real hard-core stuff – but I said, no way. I wasn't having none. Too dodgy.'

Carol could almost have kissed his disgusting mouth. She copied down the number with a shaking hand then cleared her throat. 'This Jones, tell me what he looks like.'

'Oh, I can do better than that,' said Runsmith. The grin was now spread wide and brimmed with self-satisfaction. He could hardly contain himself. 'I can give you a photograph.' Carol continued to smile back as though he were her best friend, as he reached into his pocket again, drew out an envelope, held it up teasingly, and awaited her grateful applause. He was a total shit who should have come forward earlier, but Carol kept smiling her warmest smile as she held out a trembling hand to accept this manna from heaven.

The team in the murder room were transfixed before the computer screen. Linda's photograph was not as bad as some of the others. She was not engaged in copulation, fellatio or buggery. She was wearing a gymslip, pulled down to bare her breasts and she was leaning forward provocatively, cupping them in her hands as though offering them to the onlooker. 'Sarah, the saucy schoolgirl wants you', said the caption. 'But she needs some strict discipline first!'

'It's her!' exclaimed Bridgeman, smashing one fist into the other. 'It's bloody well her!'

Doggie cleared his throat. 'Do you think,' he asked tentatively, 'that this means she could still be alive?'

That wiped the smile from Bridgeman's face. He shook his head sadly, 'Not a hope. Be too dodgy, wouldn't it? If she is, they'll be waiting for an opportunity to get rid of her.' He sighed. 'But I doubt it. I do really doubt it. I think she's a goner.'

'You never know,' said Doggie, determinedly upbeat for some strange reason. 'She might still be on the premises when they've tracked the subscriber down.'

The Met DI had said they were on the trail of the person who placed the pictures.

Bridgeman shook his head sadly. 'You know how long these things can take. Like the man said, you think you've got them, then the trail goes cold and they disappear into the ether again.'

He looked at his watch. Oh God, it was half-past one. Hannah! He rang The Goat but she had gone.

Subconsciously, Jenny had been waiting for the good times to end. Robin's new-found enthusiasm for her and their plans would inevitably wane. But it hadn't. Reached a plateau, perhaps. Calmed down a little, maybe. Become more grounded in reality. But his inclination towards the larger gesture still remained. 'Thinking big' he always called it – and hadn't that trait paid off for him early on in his career? Mind you, she smiled to herself, his current ambitions were scarcely on the same scale. Much more domestic. She should be grateful for that. And she was.

'Look' – Robin tapped the table with his pen – 'I realize that a glossy finish costs more, but. . . .' More tapping, but now in time with the words. 'We must have a decent product to launch Rojen Cards.'

'I know, but it's the cost of that big a print run which worries me most.'

'Darling,' he said, 'there's no point in just getting a small number printed – the return per card will be pathetic.' He pointed to the price list. 'Why pay a hundred and twenty-seven pounds for only a hundred when for a few quid more – only a hundred and eighty-six – you can get a thousand!'

'But we haven't got "only a hundred and eighty-six pounds" and the VAT has to go on top of that!'

'You don't understand, do you? We have to speculate to—'

'I know, I know.' She changed tack before he became disheartened and sulky. 'I know,' she said brightly, 'we could raise the capital by selling something.' She held up her left hand, displaying her mother's diamond ring.

'Oh, no. I'm not having that!'

'I don't see why not? It's only a thing.'

'I'll humble myself with the bank manager first,' he said dramatically.

They looked at each other, stalemated. The phone rang, Robin grabbed the receiver.

'Well, hi, Herbie!' he exclaimed after a pause. Herbie Strong, an ex-colleague. 'No?' exclaimed Robin. 'You're joshing! Jacko? Well, I'm blowed.'

Their conversation became even more animated.

'Do you think so? Really?' The answer, obviously, was yes. 'Brilliant!' enthused Robin. 'Fantastic! What? Now?' He glanced at his watch. 'Well' – he looked guiltily at Jenny then at his watch again – 'I could do it in just under the hour.'

It transpired that account executive, Jacko Robinson, had quit at a vital moment in a baby-food campaign. Headhunted, it was suspected. The company, Robin's old company, were desperate for an instant replacement. Robin not only knew the people on the campaign, he also knew the client, and he had handled a couple of baby-food ads in his time. The market was a specialized one and very competitive. Herbie, the great, wonderful Herbie, was of the opinion that this was the moment for Robin's renaissance as a top advertising supremo – he actually talked like that. More, he'd trailed the idea with the powers-that-be and they were willing to see Robin. But speed was of the essence both to take over the account and before some other likely candidate got wind of it.

Robin told Jenny all this in a rush and added that he had to leave immediately.

'But you've got to wait until a police officer gets here!' Jenny insisted, the old panic rising in her throat.

'I *can't*, sweetie. It's got to be now, Herbie says, or never. This is my chance!' He was lit up. All the spark and fervour were back. She'd imagined him content before, but now knew differently. He had only decided to make the best of a bad job because he'd had no choice.

'Why not come into town with me? Do a bit of shopping. . . .'

'I *can't*. You know I've got to finish Mrs Danewick's hyacinth picture. I'm late with it already – and we need the money!'

'You won't have to do any more commissions after today!' he assured her, grandly. Then, seeing her strained expression, he said, 'Look, ring the police now. By the time I've had a quick smarten-up they'll be well on their way. Probably will have got here. And, let's face it, the bogey-man is hardly likely to be outside in the woods, waiting to pounce the minute I leave, is he, sweetie?'

Of course, Robin was right.

22

Jenny could hear Robin dashing about upstairs from bedroom to bathroom and back again. She envisaged him, wings on his feet, splashing in and out of the shower, giving himself a lightning shave, flinging lashings of cologne about then changing into his slick, new, blue-black, high-collared suit. Successful admen were wearing nothing else, he had informed her, when justifying the outrageous outlay.

She must snap out of this daze and ring Carol. Just as she was reaching for the receiver the phone rang. Damn. Well, she would tell whoever it was to ring her back in a minute.

'Hi, Jenny,' said a cheerful, dark-brown, male voice. David!

'Good heavens, I thought you'd left the country.' She was pleased she managed to sound laid back and nonchalant while her pulse told a different story.

He chuckled. 'Not exactly, but when I came for my lesson I found half the local police force were dashing down your little lane. So I reckoned it was not a good time for a painting lesson.'

'You were right there!' she admitted. 'Aerial perspective was far from my mind I can tell you.'

His voice became more serious. 'I was so worried when I saw all those boys in blue. Are you all right?'

'Yes, I'm OK now, thanks. It was pretty horrible at the time though. Terrifying in fact,' she admitted. Ridiculous for her to feel so happy at the sound of his voice and warmed because he had been worried about her!

'They told me you found a body and it turns out to be Furness!' he exclaimed. 'I couldn't believe it!'

'Yes. Incredible isn't it?' She was about to tell him that the police were suspicious that he knew more than he was saying, but stopped – what if the phone was tapped?

'Well, maybe we'll be able to catch up on things soon because the reason I'm ringing is that I'd like to resume our lessons. Would that be all right? If you're recovered enough?'

Would it! 'Yes.' She kept it casual. 'Sure. A little distraction would do me good. When do you want to come?'

'I was wondering,' he said tentatively, 'whether I might pop around now. If you're free, that is?'

'Now!'

'Well, pretty soon. In about half an hour or so. That's if Robin wouldn't mind?'

'Oh, he won't be here,' she said without thinking. 'He's going out. But. . . .'

'Rather not?'

'No, well . . . it's just that. . . .'

'I understand. Short notice. Cheeky of me really.'

Oh, why not? She'd have plenty of time to finish Mrs Danewick's painting later on. Maybe she could even demonstrate on it for David. 'No, that's fine. You come along.'

'Sure? I don't want to be a nuisance.'

'Yes. Absolutely.' Robin would be gone in five minutes. Plenty of time for her to tidy herself up.

'My painting arm is in desperate need of exercise!'

She laughed. He was so cheerful. Such a tonic. 'I look forward to it,' she said, still trying to keep the tone fairly formal, but failing.

She put down the phone. No need to ring Carol just yet then. She'd do it when David arrived. That would be plenty of time.

Carol dashed into the murder room, flourishing her notebook and exclaiming, 'You won't believe what I've got!'

'You won't believe what we've got either,' retorted Glass in, for him, an enthusiastic tone. He tipped his head towards the screen which was still exhibiting Linda's provocative photograph. 'I suppose you can't exactly call it good news,' he admitted, 'ghastly, in fact. But it might get us somewhere at last.'

Carol halted her dash before the screen to gaze tight-lipped. 'The bastards,' she said vehemently, 'the fucking bastards! She's only a child.' She shot a glance at Bridgeman. 'Does this mean . . . do you think. . . ?'

'She could be alive?' He shook his head sadly. 'I really don't think so . . . and even if she is we're probably miles from tracking them down.' He paused. 'So, what's your news?'

She held out her notebook absently, her eyes still glued to the screen. It could be Jackie up there for all the world to gloat at! 'A telephone number.'

'Oh, right,' said Bridgeman, trying not to sound too deflated. 'I thought at least you'd got a serial murder confession out of him.'

'It's the telephone number of the man who hired Jake Runsmith to take photographs of the girls,' she retorted.

That made them sit up and shut up. Bridgeman grabbed the notebook. 'What's more,' Carol raised her voice and looked around with a superior air, 'I have a photograph of the mysterious, missing man, the fake Furness.'

All sound in the murder room ceased apart from the background hum of a dozen motherboards. Every eye was clamped on Carol and the print she waved aloft.

'Bloody hell,' said Bridgeman. 'A breakthrough.'

The telephone number belonged to B. Jones, Flat 9, Hadley Court, Carding Street, Mayfair – which tied up with Jenny's sighting of the man she thought might be Furness. She had seen him turning off Bond Street which – judging by the A–Z – was no distance from Carding Street.

'Loath as I am to get into bed with the Met,' muttered Glass, 'I think we need a bit of inter-force co-operation here.'

DI Weathers of the Porn Squad was elated that his quarry might be in sight. His own trail had gone cold again.

'We'll stake it out straight away,' he said.

'I'd rather you didn't,' said Glass. 'I don't want them warned off.'

'Yeah, but what if your snout has tipped them off that he was going to spill.'

The man had a point.

'Discreet obbo, mate,' Weathers assured him. 'Softly, softly and all that.'

'Please do be careful,' said Glass. 'I can't stress how important this is to us.'

'No worries.'

Was the man Australian or something? Or was that just weird Metspeak?

'DS Bridgeman will be up there in about forty minutes.'

'If the birds do start to fly, shall we bring them down?'

Glass pondered. Risk-taking time. 'Yes, please do.'

Jenny touched on a little soft pink lipstick and pinned up her hair. Then she took it down again. He was a natural man, he must prefer natural looks. Sultana scones were waiting a warm through on top of the Aga. Time to relax. She didn't want to seem flustered or eager when he arrived.

She got out her paints, filled her water pots, grabbed a handful of kitchen paper with which to stem any watercolour overruns and sat down at her easel.

As the silence settled around her she glanced up at the kitchen windows. They were all reflections and dark shadows and shapes now, the light was fading so fast. Was that one a human shape? Was someone standing out there watching her?

You've been foolish again, she chastized herself. What if David is delayed? Or if he goes home early? He didn't say how long he was going to stay. She reached for the phone, muttering to herself, 'You should have done this earlier, you silly cow! Given them time to arrange a substitute guard.'

The phone was dead. She rattled at the rest – nothing. Oh, hell. Someone *was* looking in on her, she knew it! She took a deep breath, striving to quell her rising panic. What should she do?

'Think woman. Think!'

Her mobile phone was in the car. That's where she always used it, so that's where it stayed. How stupid! Well, there was nothing for it.

'You've got to get it!'

She stole another glance out into the darkness. It was almost solid now. Once outside these locked doors she was totally vulnerable. But what else could she do? The panic button! That was it! They'd told her not to hesitate to hit it. She jumped up, relieved, and marched into the hall. Her hand was reaching out towards the silver button half-hidden by the door curtain, then she held back. Just what was she going to say when half the force came roaring in, leaving other, vitally important cases – 'Sorry, I was frightened of the dark.'? She could just imagine Sergeant Bridgeman's face – full of contempt and what if he arrived when David was here!

There was nothing for it. She had to get the mobile. It would only take a matter of seconds, for heaven's sake. She tapped out the sequence on the kitchen table: '*Quietly*, unlock the front door. Dash out, car key ready. Open the car door. Snatch the mobile from the front well. Then back again'. She took a deep breath, put her hand on the door key, then stopped. She would go in a minute. When she had really got her breath back. David might arrive soon and make her journey unnecessary.

'You can see there's money in the porn business,' said Bridgeman, nodding at the glistening glass frontage of Hadley Court. Each huge pane was clamped on to the next with sleek, brushed-gold bolts which glowed under the street lights. Beyond the glass: a forest of greenery fringing a half-circle of black marble – the reception desk. Behind this grand counter they could just make out the hall porter. He was a big man, done up like a Ruritanian general in a dark-green uniform and cap garnished with gold braid.

'No argument there,' agreed DI Weathers. 'It's a paying game.'

'There *is* somebody in flat 9,' said Mike, a plump-faced and rather sweaty young detective constable. 'We've spotted them moving about.'

'Them?' queried Bridgeman.

'Could be just one,' Mike admitted. 'Hard to tell with all that drapey stuff at the windows.'

Bridgeman was keeping his eyes on the hall porter who, every now and then, stood up and emerged from behind the desk to wander across the white marble floor and peer out of the glass wall frontage. He was a very big man.

'So, what's the plan?' he asked.

'We'll just steam in,' said Weathers, cheerfully. 'Mike, here, will kneecap that fellow and we'll dash up to the flat. Jane will belt around the back – there's a tradesman's entrance and a stairway to the garage there. You and I' – he patted Bridgeman on the shoulder – 'will do our John Wayne act and breach the stockade.' He looked at Bridgeman. 'I have sent for more back-up. Do you want to wait?'

Bridgeman shook his head. 'No, let's go.'

'I am tooled up, by the way.' Weathers patted the left side of his chest. 'Just in case.'

It was time. She had to go now. Jenny held her breath, opened the front door as quickly as she could and ran towards the car. The porch light sprang on, putting her centre stage for any watcher to see, but making her progress easier and quicker. She was at the car, key ready, reaching for the lock with a shaky hand.

As she tried to insert the key, it slipped, the key case fell out of her grasp, hit the ground and tumbled under the car. She swore, got down on her knees, scrabbling about on the wet gravel. Got it! She grasped the key case tightly, filling her nails with muck and grit and brought it up and towards the lock. There was a crackling sound on the gravel, behind her. Oh, God!

'Need some assistance, miss?' asked a deep, male voice.

She turned her head very slowly, the terror tightening her throat. Then, in seconds, sheer relief. 'Oh David, David!' she gasped, clutching his chest. 'You gave me such a shock. Thank God it's you!'

Bridgeman was dashing across Hadley Court's shiny, marble floor towards the mirrored lift. They'd nailed the porter while he was away from the reception desk, grabbed duplicate keys from his board, and left the big man, surprisingly, cowering under Mike's threatening eye. Bridgeman was still fearful that he could have some covert method of warning Flat 9, or that the occupants might have look-outs on duty. Big money bought big protection.

'Come on! Come on!' he grated as the lift trundled its way down – then stopped at the first floor.

'I'll take the stairs,' yelled Weathers.

At last, the lift reached the ground floor – and went straight past to the basement and car-park. Damn, they'd not covered that lift exit. Too late, now. The lift was back and he got in.

Bridgeman emerged on the third floor, opposite Flat 8, just as a breathless DI Weathers rounded the corner into the corridor. Together, they crept towards Flat 9. With great care Weathers inserted the key, desperately trying to prevent the huge, brass key-tag from banging on the door frame. He thumped on the door, shouted, 'Police, open the door!' turned the key and pushed. They were in.

'Let's go inside,' said David, grasping Jenny's arm. 'It would be better there.'

She laughed. 'Well, I certainly can't teach you about wet-in-wet out here!'

'I think you'll find,' he said, his grasp tightening, 'that the teaching is going to be all the other way this time.'

Jenny looked at him questioningly, but his expression was blank. This has to be some sort of joke, she thought, as he marched her towards the doorway. He would let her in on it, in a minute and they would both laugh.

As he continued pushing and propelling her into the house, she lost patience and exclaimed, 'Hey, let go of me! You're hurting! The joke's gone far enough.'

He squeezed her arm even tighter and laughed derisively. 'A joke? Is that what you think this is? He looked her up and down with narrowed, contemptuous eyes. 'You silly cow!'

Jenny thought she must be going mad. This couldn't be gentle, caring David looking at her with such disdain and saying such terrible things.

'But, you're my friend. I can't believe ... this is ridiculous.' She managed a trembling smile. 'I know. It's a sort of April fool – or something. Isn't it?'

He stood looking at her, his head on one side, then slowly began shaking it. 'Sorry, ducky,' he grinned, wolfishly. 'You're out of luck.'

She stood stock still. If she didn't move, nothing would happen.

He watched her greedily, obviously revelling in her fear. Feeding off it. Eventually he spoke. 'You women,' he spat, 'so stupid. So hypocritical. You've been begging for it long enough.'

Those words again! She couldn't believe she was hearing those words again!

He began to move towards her, slowly raising his arms. 'I'm glad you put on something special for me. More fun ripping it off.'

The downstairs panic button was in the hall. Her back was towards the door which led there. Was it open? Could she reach it before he grabbed her?

'Robin ... will be back any minute,' she stammered.

He stopped and smiled. 'No. I don't think so. You wouldn't have invited me if he was, would you now?' He laughed again. 'And, of course, you *did* invite me. The police already know you invited me here regularly. Bored, neglected housewife. Begging for it. Any jury would be more than convinced when I tell them how you seduced me. Almost against my will it was. But I felt

189

sorry for you. You were *more than* consenting though – you were eager.' The smile had gone now. He began to move towards her again.

'They're after you, the police,' she said, stealing a quick glance towards the door. It was slightly ajar. 'About the murder.'

That stopped him for a moment. Then he shrugged. 'Know nothing about it, do I? I'm only the poor bloody gardener, after all.' He had dropped his arms and was swinging them slowly back and forth, fists clenched. 'And don't even think about dashing for that door. You haven't got a chance. We're alone. Nobody can save you.' He was hissing now, loving every moment. 'The more you resist, the more you'll bloody suffer.' He held up his right arm flexing his fingers in and out of a tight fist. She knew that this dragging it out, talking to terrify her, was all part of his pleasure. He's going to kill me, she realized.

Somehow, the knowledge released her. Fury rose within her. How dare he! She was going to go down fighting. Not whimpering. She turned and ran for the hall door.

23

The flat was spacious and rambling, Bridgeman realized, once through the door. They had burst straight into a long narrow hallway lined with gilt-framed pictures and mirrors. To either side, halfway down, were doors. Both were closed so they headed straight for the lighted, open room at the far end of the hall where a male voice was bellowing, 'You haven't foxed me!' The television game show audience roared its response – which helped to cover their approach.

They cannoned into a large, square room, resplendent with ornate, French repro furniture, but Bridgeman's eyes were riveted on the startled man leaping up from a large crimson settee. He was an awesome sight. Almost as wide as he was tall and all muscle. The massive shoulders and shaven head were thrust forward, the expression ferocious – and he was speeding straight for them. If he was a martial arts expert they could be in dead trouble.

'Don't even think about it, sunshine!' bellowed Weathers, thrusting out his warrant card as if it were some sort of magic talisman. 'I'll charge you with things you've never bloody heard of – and murder will just be the start!' He was reaching into his inside pocket as he spoke.

The man slowed, uncertain. His eyes darted about wildly, particularly past them, to the way out. Was it worth chancing his luck?

'You lot stay there, Sergeant Mannings,' yelled Weathers to a non-existent officer outside the flat, 'and draw your weapons.' He glared at man mountain, blew his nose on the handkerchief he had taken from his pocket, and added, 'There are some very funny people about.'

Bridgeman thought that 'draw your weapons' was over-egging the pudding a bit, but he joined in the charade by speaking into his radio, 'OK, Dougie, we're in. The rest of you can come up now.'

The hulk realized that he had hesitated too long and stood sullenly defeated, his arms hanging loosely by his side. Weathers switched off the television. 'Where,' he enquired menacingly, 'are the girls?'

The man stared hard at them. He took a deep breath then thrust his head in the direction of a door at the back of the room. 'In there. And it's nothing to do with me.'

This was the moment. It was now or never! Jenny ran for the door to the hall and was through it almost to the front door and the panic button when she felt David's weight behind her. He grasped the hand she was thrusting towards the button and twisted it till she screamed with pain.

'You stupid woman!' he yelled into her ear ferociously. 'Stupid, stupid, stupid!' She was aware of a sharp crack. Had her wrist snapped? David pushed even more heavily on her and they both collapsed on to the floor, his whole weight crushing her. She was trapped. She could not move and could scarcely breathe. Why was he doing that? What was the point? There was no escaping.

Then she realized he wasn't moving. Had he had a heart attack or something? Or was this another of his evil games? She began to push him, trying to tilt him on his side so she could wriggle out from under. He didn't stop her, but her hands were slipping. They were wet and sticky. She was half out and had his body on its side. Then it fell backwards, away from her. As it did, she saw a scarlet trickle bubbling from his mouth.

'Didn't expect to see *him* here,' said a smooth, male voice. 'The gardener! Give me strength.'

Jenny stared upwards, then suddenly recognized the face. 'Mr Furness! Oh, thank God it's you! He's been trying to. . . .' Her voice faded away.

He had a revolver in his hand that was the crack she had heard, and now it was pointing at her. 'I know you're not going to believe this,' he muttered, 'but I don't really enjoy killing women.'

She was enraged. Summoning all her strength she dived for his legs. He was taken unawares and stumbled and fell head-long. Seizing her chance she jumped up and dashed for the stairs. She heard him struggling to regain his feet in the spreading blood and cursing as he slid and slipped. Jenny didn't look back from the top of the stairs but ran for the bedroom where the other panic button was situated. The handle refused to revolve in her slimy grasp! Oh God, don't say *this* door was locked. She grabbed the corner of her blouse, wrapped it around the handle and turned. It opened. As she slammed the door shut behind her she could hear him stumbling and swearing his way up the stairs. With a strength she never knew she had, she dragged an antique chest of drawers towards the door, gave it an almighty push and it toppled over, crashing and splintering deafeningly as it hit the floor. She rammed it hard against the door then turned to reach behind the bed and bang on the panic button again and again.

'I've pressed the panic button,' she shouted. 'The police will be here any minute!'

'Don't be so stupid.' he yelled back. 'I've disabled them. I'm not a fool!' He was grappling with the bloodied door handle and having the same trouble as she. Then he had it and began to push. The chest of drawers moved forwards – but only a little. She pushed back. She needed more weight. Desperately she looked back around the room. The bed was too large and she could hardly lift that on top of the tumbled chest – it would have to be that dressing-table. But dare she leave off resisting his push for long enough to fetch it? She would have to be quick, very quick. Fear and rage were still driving her on. She dragged the dressing-table towards the door, then gave it a tremendous push so that it too crashed over, to lay suspended half on and half off the upturned chest. She tried to drag it into a better position but it was too unwieldy. At least it added weight. He was barging now.

Then all movement stopped. What was he up to? She soon knew. A sharp, explosive crack rang out as a splintered hole appeared halfway up the door. He was shooting through the door! She crouched low behind her barrier. If he carried on firing he must get her in the end.

'You know you can't win!' he shouted. Her crouching position prevented Jenny from getting sufficient purchase to resist further. The piled furniture began to inch inwards.

The girls were alive. Bridgeman gazed wonderingly from one to the other. They were made up like painted dolls and were wearing skimpy, provocative lingerie. But they were alive. He tried not to cry. When their posse had crashed their way into the locked bedroom, the girls had been cowering fearfully against the wall, clinging desperately to each other.

'It's all right, it's all right. We're police,' Bridgeman assured them as he beckoned the young WPC into the room.

Linda and Cynthia stood, trembling, and stared at them disbelievingly. Then they collapsed, sobbing, back into each other's arms.

'Your parents are going to be very glad to see you,' Bridgeman murmured, thinking, as he said it, that it had to be the most banal and obvious statement he had ever made. He didn't care.

'Congrats, mate,' said Weathers, patting Bridgeman on the shoulder. 'Good result. Marvellous. Bloody marvellous.'

Baxter, the thug who had been guarding the girls, had begun to talk. In fact, he was singing like the proverbial canary. Most of the words were interspersed with the familiar refrain, 'You gotta believe me. I had nothing to do with it.'

Bridgeman assumed his most understanding persona. He sometimes wondered how many utterly vile people have their own vision of themselves as innocent victims of circumstances, verified by police in this way, when someone ought to be telling them what evil bastards they were.

'These things do happen,' he shrugged. 'You get caught up in things. . . . Help us, and we'll do what we can for you,' he added with disarming sincerity.

'You've got the picture, I guess,' the man said nonchalantly, as he felt about his bulk for a cigarette. Bridgeman leaned forward and offered him one. 'Girls wanting to be models, hooked by Furness and Jones, then persuaded to do a bit of "figure work" as they call it – all for their portfolios, of course.' He grinned knowingly at Bridgeman. 'Then, next thing is, it all goes a little bit further. Jones is a good-looking bloke. Very persuasive. More photos – and so on.'

'A girl was killed,' said Bridgeman, quietly.

Baxter shook his head slowly. 'Stupid accident. Nothing to do with me. They'd given her some drugs, then a couple of blokes is having a go at her. They told me she just stopped breathing.'

'Strangled,' said Bridgeman. 'She was strangled.'

Baxter paused and took a long drag at his cigarette. His hand was trembling.

'Right,' he said. 'Same thing, isn't it?'

Bridgeman bit his tongue. No point. 'And Furness?'

Baxter shrugged. 'Got windy. Wanted out. He was getting panicky – dangerous like. Jones said, no way.'

'And he was topped in the locked room?'

Baxter frowned. 'Locked room? Oh, yeh. In the upstairs room. Yeh. It all got a bit messy – so it was locked till they could get down to clean it up – had to wait until the bird, you know, the one who was looking after the place, went out. At least, that's what they told me. Nothing to do with me.'

'No, of course not.' Bridgeman paused. 'You haven't mentioned the other bloke.'

'What other bloke?'

'The gardener.'

He shrugged. 'Don't know nothing about him.'

'Young man. Good-looking. Dark, curly hair.'

He shook his head and grimaced. 'Don't ring no bells.'

'All right. So, where can we find this Jones? This pretend Mr Furness? Where's he gone?'

Baxter looked nervous. 'I dunno,' he said firmly. He was rubbing the side of his nose with his finger and his eyes were wandering. Bridgeman suddenly knew where Jones had gone.

'Yes, you bloody do!' he exclaimed, getting to his feet. 'And you'd better tell us. *Now!*'

'He just said he was off to clear up a a bit of business,' said Baxter.

Bridgeman was on him like a tiger. He grasped Baxter by the collar and wrenched back his head. 'Where?' he yelled. 'Bloody, where?'

'Berry Hill House,' muttered Baxter.

Jenny didn't know what else to do. Should she keep pushing against her pile of furniture in the vain hope she could stop the inevitable breakthrough? Or should she take a chance and leave off for a few moments, to gather more weight for her blockade? But what else could she use? All that was left was the king-size bed and the contents of the built-in wardrobe. The bed was a massive wooden affair, too big and too heavy for her to shift and what good would a lot of clothes be? Maybe if she dumped them on top of the pile they would add a little weight and give any bullets another layer to pass through, she thought, desperately.

No. Got to try to move the bed. She'd dash from her post in spurts, edging it across a little at a time but she'd better hurry.

'You might as well give up!' he panted. 'I'll be through any minute.'

She didn't answer.

'Come out now and I'll make it easier for you,' he offered. 'A quick death.'

'Oh, well, thanks a bunch!' she yelled. What a liberty! 'I'll go down fighting if it's all the same to you.' She hated those films where the female victim just gave up, hands on face, waiting to be strangled.

Rugs. There was a thick, five foot long, pink-and-cream rug half under her feet, and the bed rested on a huge Persian carpet. Heaving and sweating, she managed to extricate the smaller rug without actually leaving her post. It proved amazingly heavy but comforting as a blockade extra. Backwards and forwards, pulling and pushing, she dragged it half over the pile and managed to jam it in across the doorway. Then she made two rushes to the wardrobe grabbing piles of the heavier winter clothes. She jammed these around and above the rug to impede his progress if he broke through. Nonetheless, as he barged again, her furniture pile made a sudden leap towards her. She would have to try for the bed.

She dashed over, grabbed the bedposts and put all her might into giving the bottom of the bed a hefty shove. It didn't move an inch. She tried again – heaving and shoving. No response. She went back to her barricade. Now she really did begin to feel defeated. What else was there left for her to do? Nothing.

You can give it your last shot to try to push him back, that's what you can do, she told herself. She took a deep breath and gave an almighty shove. Her fear and fury seemed to give her a strength she didn't know she had. She was going forward! Just a little, an inch or so but. . . . She heaved again. More progress! A couple more shoves and the door would be closed! It was! She couldn't believe it. The curved feet of the upturned dressing-table supported her as, fighting to get her breath back, she stared at the closed door and listened. Not a sound. Total silence. She tried to still her panting so she could hear better. No difference.

What the hell was going on? Had he given up and left? Why should he? Who was going to disturb him? Should she take this opportunity to have another shot at moving the bed and the huge carpet it lay on? But was that what he wanted? Her to be diverted, so he could make the final breakthrough? What was he up to? Was he trying another approach? Her gaze went towards the window and she trembled. This uncertainty was more frightening than the previous reality.

24

Bridgeman was breaking all the speed limits, taking wild risks in a manner quite alien to him. Why had he not insisted that Jenny move out? Was he mad allowing her to stay in that house? He should have seen this coming!

Don't panic, Robin will be there to help protect her, had been his first reaction when he heard that Jones was heading for Berry Hill House, and they have alarm buttons. Then it sank in: what use was one untrained man and panic buttons against an armed and determined villain? At least the nick had some good news. There had been no frantic phone messages and the buttons had not been activated. They promised to send in the cavalry ASAP, including the helicopter. Then he rang Berry Hill House and found that the phone was dead.

A red-faced man in a black Audi shouted soundlessly and gesticulated wildly at him as slipped through a narrow gap to get ahead. Why was he doing this when it was probably too late? The phone was dead. *She* must be dead. He screeched to a halt at red traffic lights, revving the engine and willing them to change.

His mobile rang. It was Carol.

'Is she all right?' he shouted.

'I don't know,' she admitted.

'You don't bloody know?'

'We can't get through by road.' She sounded breathless. 'RTA. A bloody great pile-up.'

He banged on the steering wheel. 'I don't believe this!'

'We're continuing on foot.' Her breath was coming faster now. She sounded as if she was running.

'But the chopper? That's got to be there by now?'

'Grounded,' she gasped. 'Fault. Out of action.'

He wanted to bellow with frustration.

'Don't kill yourself getting there,' she panted. Her words were breaking up. 'And, don't forget. He's armed. We're armed.' Her voice strengthened to the approximation of a shout. 'But *you're* not!' The line went dead.

The silence was getting to Jenny. She was exhausted, and the terror was back. What was his next move going to be? Climbing up the outside walls to the window? But he'd need a ladder and that would make him vulnerable and noisy. She stopped. No, of course, it needn't. He could climb out of the window of the next bedroom along and to this one. Couldn't he? She had no idea if the ledge was wide enough for him to edge along but, again, he would be vulnerable. She could shove him off the ledge. But not if his gun was pointed at her!

She peered out from one side of the window into the darkness but could see nothing. She shivered. He could be close by – almost there! She sank back down on to the floor and racked her brains. 'Think, think, think, woman!' The silence was threatening to overwhelm her. She wanted nothing more than to curl up into a self-protective ball. Suddenly, she leaped to her feet. She knew what was happening! He'd gone to find a makeshift battering ram to smash through the door and her pathetic blockade. She should be using this time to reinforce it with the bed and the carpet.

She froze again. If he was going to come through the window, wouldn't she just be reinforcing her *tomb*? She had sudden flashes of black-garbed, SAS men, silently abseiling from above, crashing through windows, throwing smoke bombs and stun grenades and efficiently wiping out the terrorists inside. That was how he would do it. And what could she do to resist? Nothing.

She felt defeated but somehow relieved. She had fought hard and could do nothing more. A faint smell made her wrinkle her nose. Faint, but acrid and it was growing stronger. Was he trying to gas her? As it thickened, she realized. Fire! He was going to smoke her out and shoot her, or watch her go up in flames.

Jenny flew to the windows. They were double glazed, she remembered with horror. To her relief, one of the interior panes slid back easily. She reached for the latch on the outside window, released it and pushed. Nothing happened. Stiff with paint? She pushed harder. It was solid. The smell was getting stronger, catching her throat, causing her eyes to stream. She could hear the flames crackling and spitting. She must get out! The dressing-chest stool was a flimsy object but it did have long, strong legs. Battering the pane had no effect whatsoever. The stool bounced off not even cracking the glass. Panic lent power to her arms. She smashed frantically at the resistant pane, cursing and swearing as she did so. Cursing and swearing at Robin. It was *his* fault. What sort of a man was he to leave her to die like this? Alone and terrified. A minute splinter mark appeared. More hammering and it changed to a crack, then, suddenly, the window disintegrated.

The frame was small and the fragments around the edges were going to tear her to pieces but anything was better than being slowly suffocated or burned to death. Being shot, even. Her coughing nearly choked her and she could not see for tears. The flames were licking around the door frame. She pulled herself up on to the windowsill and crouched there looking down into the blackness. God, what a fool! She needed a rope! She had half-turned back when she felt a searing, knife-like pain in her right shoulder, lost her grip and fell backwards into the room. Another knife, this time in her head. She felt no more.

Carol's lungs were about to burst. She had never run for so long before. Distance had never been her forte and a dark and uneven country lane was no substitute for Tartan track. She was keeping up with the lads very well, anxiety for Jenny driving her on and on. But it was no good, once around the next corner she just had to stop to get her breath. The sight that greeted them as they turned practically stopped them in their tracks anyway. Lighting up the moonless night were the flames from Berry Hill House eerily interspersed with spiralling plumes of smoke. Spurred on to a last great effort, though with a heavy heart, Carol thought, what hope now for Jenny?

As they panted around the final bend they saw the fire had taken hold up to the roof at the rear but had not yet reached the front upper storey. Through the smoke Carol spotted a man climbing a ladder leading to a smashed window in the master bedroom. There was no sign of anyone inside trying to get out. What was this? A desperate Jones making sure his quarry had been annihilated? The climber had almost reached the open window when through the noise of crackling fire and the exploding of timbers came a sharper crack. The dark figure stopped and swayed, desperately hanging on to the ladder which was threatening to topple sideways. Another sharp crack and he fell, limply and awkwardly, like a doll discarded from a pram.

Somewhere behind her came a commanding shout, 'Armed police. Drop your weapon!' The gunman obviously did not obey. Three or four shots in quick succession were followed by a silence, broken only by the noises of the fire.

Carol ran past the gunman's body to the fallen man. The shock of recognition almost stunned her as she knelt. Blood was gurgling from his mouth. He was trying to say something but she couldn't catch it. She crouched down and put her ear to his mouth. Just hissing noises. Then she made out, 'Je . . . Jen. . . .' A sudden gush of blood began to choke him but he made one final effort. She just caught, 'Up . . . up there,' before Robin died.

Bridgeman entered the mortuary and went to look at the body of Jones.

'You'd better come and see this,' said Reg Hailey, the pathologist, beckoning him over to where David, the gardener, lay. He pointed to the man's eyes. 'Look. one blue and one brown.' He lifted up the tumbling curls. 'And his blond roots are starting to show through.'

Bridgeman stared for several seconds, seemingly hypnotized by that ice-blue eye, still coldly evil, even in death. Eventually, he whispered, 'Bloody hell!'

'Of course, this one is a coloured contact lens.' Hailey continued, pointing to the brown eye. The other one's fallen out. 'Bloody good these days, aren't they?'

'I never even *suspected*,' whispered Bridgeman. 'She said he was dark and. . . .'

'No reason why.' Hailey stopped and looked at the sergeant. 'I've got a feeling I'm missing something here. Are you about to enlighten me?'

'It's Hayden!' exclaimed Bridgeman. 'Bloody Hayden.'

'Ah. Right,' murmured Hailey, nodding.

'He was a vicious rapist who got away with it!' exclaimed Bridgeman angrily.

Hailey gave him a sideways look, then patted his hand. 'Hasn't got away with it this time, has he?'

'No,' said Bridgeman. 'He hasn't, has he?' And he smiled.

The smell had changed. It was no longer acrid but a curious mixture of antiseptic, herbs and citrus. Gingerly, Jenny lifted her eyelids a fraction then closed them again, instantly. Sunshine was agonizing, she decided. The herby, citrussy smell began to dominate and, when she forced herself to open her eyes again, she realized what it was. After-shave – but not Robin's. A solid male figure by her bed was leaning forward wafting it towards her.

'Hi,' said Bridgeman softly. 'Nice day.'

She tried to move her lips but nothing happened and the movement sent a stinging pain into her right temple, causing her grief again. He really was an impossible man. Her head pounded sickeningly. She tried to reach up to feel her forehead but an agonizing pain shot through her right shoulder. She peered across at it wonderingly, then stretched up her other hand to touch the large dressing pad on her head. 'Ouch,' she murmured. 'That hurts.' The lips were beginning to cohese but the sound which emerged was woolly. He seemed to understand anyway.

'You received one bullet in the shoulder and another to the head.' Bridgeman spoke quietly, gently almost. 'The good news is that you must have turned your head as it struck so, instead of brain damage, or worse, you have nasty, but not life-threatening, skull bruising and a scalp wound.' He paused. 'Lucky, really.'

'Hey, that's some bedside manner you've got there, Sergeant,' she croaked.

'All that experience, terrorizing prisoners,' he retorted. They shared a rueful grin. For some reason she found his usually irritating presence immensely comforting. He was holding her hand as she slipped back into sleep.

Rolls stood there, smiling warmly, with an arm each around his wife and his stepdaughter.

'We can't thank you enough,' he said.

Bridgeman nodded acknowledgement. 'We are more than relieved I can tell you.'

'The girls are inseparable now,' Rolls went on, 'so we are sending Linda to Cynthia's school.'

'Wonderful,' said Bridgeman, wondering whether it really was such a good idea. But at least that would take some of the pressure off Linda's mum.

'And we're keeping in touch with Avril's sister,' added Mrs Rolls, 'just to give her somewhere to come back to. Hazel is such a nice girl. She'll make an older sister for them both.'

Bridgeman wondered how long this class divide would remain bridged but, what the hell, maybe he was being too cynical again.

'As a matter of interest,' said Rolls, 'was Mrs Furness involved in all this?'

Bridgeman shook his head. 'Not that we can see. It took off

after she left. Her turning up like that was merely a coincidence. The other woman, the one who made the jewellery, had gone too. She didn't stay long. Seems Mr Furness had trouble keeping his women.' He paused, then said, 'As a matter of interest, Mr Rolls, did you know that Hayden was back in this area?'

The elegant barrister shrugged. 'Not a clue. To be honest I didn't even recall the man until all this came out.'

'Just another case, was it?'

Rolls looked him straight in the eye. 'That's right, Officer.'

She was remembering now, and the fear made her tremble.

'I was on the windowsill looking down. . . .'

'I know.'

'I knew then that I was going to die.'

'But you didn't,' said Bridgeman automatically. Was there something on his mind?

'How did I . . . how did I . . . ?'

'Get out?' asked Bridgeman. 'Bloody miracle, if you ask me.'

'Don't tell me. You saved me – again.' She smiled but he failed to respond.

'No, it wasn't me this time,' he said gravely. 'Couldn't get there quickly enough.' He stared down at his fingernails, then looked up at her. 'It was Carol who got you out.'

'One thing I know for certain, it wouldn't have been that bastard Robin. He bloody well went out and left me to be killed. Did you know that?'

Bridgeman refused to meet her gaze. Eventually he murmured, 'He *did* try.'

'Try? What do you mean, try?' she retorted crossly. 'He'd gone to London. You know, the big exciting place where it all happens!' All the bitterness of her ordeal was spilling out with venom. 'Where is he now? Too embarrassed to show his face, I suppose!'

Bridgeman took a deep breath and launched into an obviously prepared speech.

'Robin came back. He saw you fall backwards into the

bedroom. The fire made the ground-floor entrances impassable so he got a ladder and started climbing. Jones saw him, shot him, and he fell.'

There was a stunned silence as Jenny took this in.

'Well, where is he then?' she said eventually. 'Is he here? In this hospital?'

Bridgeman shook his head and looked straight at her. 'He's dead. I'm so sorry.'

Jenny went back into the abyss where Bridgeman could not reach her.

Later, much later, she said, 'I don't understand. Why did he come back?'

'We don't really know. We think he must have tried to ring you. Found the phone dead, just as we did, so came back.' He paused, then ploughed on. 'Carol, and another three officers came up behind Jones just as Robin fell. They'd arrived on foot. which took Jones by surprise. More to the point, they were armed. He shot at them, they fired back. He died on the spot.' He dried her face with his handkerchief.

'It's all my fault!' she sobbed.

'I don't see how you work that out?' he said tersely.

'I should have phoned you when Robin left, but David rang and said he would come over for a lesson.'

He looked grim. 'Ah, yes – David. I was coming to that. We found his body. Obviously, Jones shot him too.' He paused, then added, 'It turns out that we were already familiar with your gardener.'

'He was going to rape me.'

Bridgeman nodded. 'It was his thing.' He was staring at the bedspread. 'I'm glad he's dead,' he whispered eventually. 'So bloody glad.'

'It's my fault! I shouldn't have encouraged him. And it's my fault Robin's dead.'

'Don't be so damn silly,' said Bridgeman briskly. 'I'm not going to let you do this again. Robin died trying to give you the gift of life. It would be wicked to throw it away with self-blame and regrets.'

'To give me. . . ? You said Carol saved me. . . .' Slowly, it dawned on her. 'He *told* her where I was?'

Bridgeman nodded and looked serious. 'Yes. Big effort. Last words. Carol went up the ladder, then one of the lads. They got you down – God knows how.'

He put his arms around her and rocked her gently back and forth. 'So it was him who saved you.'

For me, he wanted to add, but didn't. He would tell her that later. If she would listen, for once.